UNFAMILIAR MAGIC

BONNIE ELIZABETH

MY BIG FAT ORANGE CAT PUBLISHIG

Unfamliar Magic
My Big Fat Orange Cat
Mystery 2021

My Big Fat Orange Cat Publishing
MyBigFatOrangeCat.com

ISBN 978-1-953363-10-7 trade paperback

1

Running a cat café, or rather a familiar feline café, in Waverton, Kentucky should have allowed me plenty of time to spend with friends. Coming up on the second anniversary of the opening, I'd learned that wasn't always true. I'd had no idea what I was getting into when I set up my own business, no matter that I had plenty of magic to help me and plenty of friends and family to support me.

My two best friends, Natalie Edgars and Trinity Lyons, always made time to come by the café on Tuesday mornings to have coffee or tea. Like all cat cafés, our cats were in their own space behind a glass wall with several comfortable chairs, a loveseat, and a few tables for the customers who made reservations to spend time with the cats.

In the main area, I had the coffee bar, which like coffee places everywhere didn't just serve coffee. I'd talked to the local coffee shop near City Hall and the drive-through at the edge of town about what they sold the most of, and had decided on a variety of coffees, teas, and pastries. I closed sharply at 5:30. I wasn't terribly busy after four but the later hours allowed witches who wanted to visit with a potential familiar time to visit after work.

I managed the place with six employees, all part-time except for Greg who was just recently out of high school and trying to determine what he wanted to do.

That Tuesday morning, while I was on my extra-long coffee break, Greg was serving coffees along with Cade, one of my part-timers. Cade mostly covered Tuesday mornings so I could take the long break.

The coffee bar is off to the left of the room, all dark scratched wood, which had been part of the original building. Once upon a time, this place had been a tavern. The cats took up the pool room area which had always been sectioned off, so it was easy to put in the glass divider. While familiars were far more likely to remain in a set area, the health departments don't know that. In the same way, humans looked at me and saw an ordinary young businesswoman and not a witch. We keep our secrets.

The mayor loved the café because it brought in business and I have a thank-you paw print plaque on the wall near the door with my name, Jade Owlens, on it. It all looks quite normal, even if our little town in Kentucky is anything but ordinary.

Waverton is the place to go in the United States if you need a familiar or have an issue with yours. The Waverton Specialty Library holds about every book written on the subject of familiars and familiar medicine. Our three vets specialize in the problems common among familiars, from cats to horses to the occasional wild creature who is endowed with magic. We even have a college if you want to take classes and get a specialty in familiars.

We have multiple breeders, and our familiars are known world-wide. I might be from a small town in Central Kentucky, just a bit southwest of London, but I'd met folks from all over the world and even spoke four different languages—at least well enough to serve them the right coffee or tea.

I studied to be a veterinary technician right here at the college in Waverton. It's one of the most exclusive programs around. Lots of magical vet techs come here for the three-month continuing education program about working with familiars. We have several tracks for those who want to specialize. Naturally, while I was studying there, I focused on cats.

Mason, my large ginger and white bicolor male rules the roost over in the cat area of the café and keeps everyone in line. Some of the new familiars don't always get the routine, particularly not when there are ordinary folks just visiting. Mason always makes sure that all the cats are put in a position to show off their best qualities.

Sometimes I get inquiries from ordinary folks about adopting a certain familiar. Mason and I discuss the pros and cons with the cat. Some familiars say they're open to a non-magical home—it's kind of a retirement. Mostly, though, I end up sharing with the person inquiring that the cat has already been adopted out.

I've had to have my friend Natalie come in now and then to erase a memory if that person comes back and the cat hasn't been adopted. I try to stay up on things, but every now and then Mason and I get busy and it gets missed. Natalie is far better at interpersonal work like erasing memories than I am.

At any rate, that Tuesday, I was having my break from serving coffees and teas and eating a pastry with Natalie, who in addition to erasing memories, runs the hotel at the edge of town, and Trinity, my other best friend, who works for the specialty library.

Of everyone I knew, Trinity had seemed the most

unsuited to library work. She'd tended towards wildness, rebelling against authority at every opportunity. She loved being outside. Everyone expected she'd go to work at one of the farms that raised horse familiars.

Natalie is tall and blonde and has the build and harsh cheekbones suggestive of a Nordic goddess. She's outgoing and funny. She loves people, loves entertaining, and loves making sure people have a good time. The hotel is absolutely perfect for her. Her family has run it forever and she's just the latest in a long line of great hoteliers in our little town.

Trinity has dark hair and her skin is a few shades darker than either Natalie's or mine with large round eyes. Her features are softly molded as a clay sculpture. Her skin holds a softness to die for. She's quieter than Natalie, often preferring to be outside in her own company than chatting with everyone. The two of them are opposites.

I fell somewhere in the middle, though of everyone, I tend to be the most timid. I like to think I'm the peacemaker, but I could be wrong.

That morning, we had all chosen to have tea. Sometimes I have to have a latte and Natalie gets a craving for mochas now and then. Trinity loves our chai, so that's a staple for her. Today, in deference to the heat that spilling out over the state, she had it iced. It had sounded good to me so I made the same for myself. Natalie ordered a hot green tea.

Trinity and I each had a fresh-baked scone delivered from Olivia's just around the corner. That day we'd gotten thumbprint jelly scones as well as scones made with fresh peaches, and the ever-popular blueberry scones. Personally, I love the peach scones with lemon frosting. They are to die for.

"I swear Eric Boyd is going to fire me one of these days," Trinity said as she sipped her chai. She'd barely taken a bite of her blueberry scone. I smelled it from where I was sitting, the warm blueberries giving off their own scent amongst the aromas of coffee and teas. I tapped out a light beat with the instrumental music in the background.

We sat at one of the tables towards the far end of the café. If I was too visible, my employees would defer to me about decisions I wanted them to learn to make themselves, so I hid back there, in the corner on the bench that runs along that part of the wall, serving three two-top tables. Naturally, we'd pushed two of the tables together, but those two are almost always pushed together by someone.

The room held six other four-top rustic brown tables all with chairs. The bench and the chairs were all upholstered in red fabric with black and white cats on it. I'd have liked more feline variety but I'd not been able to find what I was looking for on a nice bright color like red. I also had blinds done in the same fabric. For most people, this would have been a huge expense, but my sister's magic comes from sewing and she was more than happy to make up the blinds so long as I got the fabric. She made sure I got a good deal on the cloth, too.

Her ability was lucky for me because I didn't just have blinds for the windows to the outside, but for the big wall of windows that separated the cat part of the café from the human part. Sometimes the cats needed their privacy from people. This morning, though, I had four people from out of town, all ordinary folks, enjoying some coffee with the cats. I noticed Mason had enticed Jelliane, an elderly calico to sit on a woman's lap. Good. Jelliane had been terribly depressed at the loss of her witch and she was finally starting to come out of her shell.

I shifted my feet against the dark tile floor as I listened to Trinity talk about Eric. I glanced at the walls, which were rustic wood with images of famous familiars from the town. The witches who came in often recognized some of the familiars pictured, cats or not and the ordinary folks who joined us just enjoyed the animal images.

"What happened this time?" Natalie asked. Natalie didn't understand why Trinity put up with Eric. Natalie had only ever worked for her family, starting out in housekeeping and working her way through all the positions available in a hotel. After she graduated with her business degree in hotel management in North Carolina she'd started working in management. Now she was pretty much running the place while her parents took all the trips they had always dreamed of doing.

"A book was missing from the archives," Trinity said. "It was Ezekiel Johnston's book on non-magical familiars." Trinity frowned. I did too. Familiars by nature, are magical. To have a non-magical familiar was merely a pet. If the book was kept in the archives, chances were it involved someone giving magic to an ordinary cat. A shiver went down my spine. Chances were that involved negative magic.

"Why is that your fault?" Natalie asked. I knew the rest of the conversation would be Natalie giving Trinity items to prove she'd not taken or misplaced the book. I knew Eric, though, and he wasn't the sort to listen once he made up his mind. Talk about a bad boss. I felt for Trinity. I understood that Natalie's actions were the result of her caring, but she didn't understand.

"Because I was the last one in there. I shelved a completely different book after someone asked for it from the archives." Trinity picked up her heavy cream-colored mug of chai and set it down without taking a sip. "He says he didn't let anyone else in so it had to be me. Except it wasn't. This isn't the first time he's been all over me for books that have gone missing."

Trinity was in charge of the circulation desk and she took her job seriously. She sent out fines when required. She searched out missing books. However, if Eric couldn't find something the moment he wanted it, he immediately blamed her. Even if the book was sitting on a cart waiting for one of the pages to shelve, he'd blame Trinity for the book not being back on the shelf immediately.

As the front desk person and the head library assistant, a title just below Eric's own, Trinity was only required to shelve books in the archives, where the pages weren't allowed. Some books weren't meant to be read by just anyone.

Eric was a jerk. Aunt Sharine had gone to school with him and she'd said he'd been a pompous ass back then, too.

"I think you do need to start documenting your side of these accusations," I said. "Eric may be head librarian but there is a board. And the city hires the specialty library workers. Think about it. They could make sure you got another job elsewhere in the city and then you wouldn't even lose your seniority. Besides, even if it doesn't help you, it might help the next person."

My mother had often told me that when I complained about something, I probably wasn't the only one complaining. Not everyone will step forward, so I ought to do so. Even if nothing happened, the next time someone else complained, the people in charge might listen. I didn't know if that was true, but it both supported Trinity in her belief that saying something would do nothing, but it also didn't alienate Natalie and get everyone in a huff.

This was, after all, my relaxation time and I meant to use it to enjoy my friends. If that meant I listened to Trinity's troubles, then I listened. But I did not want to end up in a fight.

"That's a good point," Natalie said, seizing on my idea. "You really do need to say something."

That's not exactly what I said. I had said Trinity needed to document things.

The bell over our door rang and I looked up to see Tom Alsez, one of Waverton's police officers, come in. He was in his full black uniform and sweat was already starting to bead on his hairline. Tom was stocky and solid and good-looking in an earthy way. My sister Julia had gone out on a few dates with him and really enjoyed his company. That was about all I knew about him, which always threw me.

Tom hadn't grown up in Waverton like so many of us.

I waved. It was always good to make sure the police know you support them when you run a business. Tom waved back. That distracted Natalie who also gave him a wave and a big smile.

For Natalie, that isn't flirting. That's just being herself. I know it can drive other women insane thinking she's interested in their partners, but she's not. I knew for a fact that she found Tom a bit annoying. Like most men, he'd definitely noticed Natalie and they'd had a few lunch dates but, to my sister's good fortune, things hadn't exactly clicked.

Trinity looked over and gave Tom a small wave as well. Tom nodded at everyone and continued to wait to get his order in. I felt a bit guilty that my employees weren't working as fast as I'd like, or so it seemed, but I wasn't giving up this particular break.

While I keep low instrumental music on in the café, something that pleases the felines, I still heard the static of his radio when he got a call.

So did Trinity and Natalie. We both looked over as he answered the call, his expression turning serious. Normally, not much happens in Waverton, but clearly, this wasn't a normal day.

Mason yowled from the feline section. I pushed Natalie's chair out of the way as I rose from the bench to find out what was going on. Through the glass, I noted that none of the ordinary people visiting had moved. The older woman with Jelliane on her lap was still there, petting the calico.

Mason was on his favorite perch near the ceiling but he wasn't laying comfortably. He was standing up, looking from cat to cat.

Jelliane had her eyes closed and her ears flattened as if she wasn't at all comfortable with what she was hearing.

I slipped into the room and headed over to Mason who leaped down into my arms. He rarely does that. The shelf is high, barely in my reach and Mason isn't a small cat.

Once there, once we were touching, I let my mind touch his.

"*What's going on?*" I asked him telepathically. Not all witches can communicate quite as easily with their familiars, but I had a knack, particularly with Mason.

"*I felt the presence of an angry, displaced spirit,*" Mason said. "*He had a familiar feel as if he's been here before. I believe someone in town has died an unnatural death.*"

I rubbed his fur, which was standing on edge, to calm him, even as an unsettling chill crept down my back. Mason's term of *unnatural death* no doubt meant someone had been murdered. Right here in Waverton.

2

When Mason had calmed, I walked back out to the table where Trinity and Natalie were still talking. Natalie raised her eyebrow slightly in question as I got to the table. I paused to give myself time to adjust from the soft soothing tans and greens of the cat area to the darker, more dramatic look of the main café. The soft music that played in the background throughout the building brought the two sections together.

I noted a couple of locals had come in. Brian Welks worked at the bank next door. He walked over every day at this time and got a plain black coffee. I think he just wanted to get out of the bank. Sarah Meyerson was getting a fancy coffee of some sort. She's definitely not a creature of habit.

Sarah ran the bookstore up the road. Naturally, she specialized in magical tomes and half the store had difficult to find books about familiars. I'd found books on familiar cat care that taught me some things I hadn't learned in class. She also had books on the advantages of various familiars.

Naturally, she carried the usual items like choosing a familiar by your astrological sign, but those were usually purchased by people from out of town. No one living here would buy into that sort of nonsense. Sarah had spells in place to keep non-magical folks from noticing the store so they didn't just wander in. Even then, she had a small selection of ordinary magic books in the front to keep them occupied, so that give she or her worker had time to do a "go away" spell on them.

I liked the way her shop smelled of old books and dust, though it made me sneeze. I sometimes went in to look through the short books she had on famous familiars. Of course, Sarah kept her familiar, Bongo, in the shop. Bongo was a five-year-old Boxer. He wasn't a typical familiar and his magic tended to have a martial edge. He probably helped with the magic to keep ordinary folks outside

Sarah had no doubt been drawn to him, not only because she needed a familiar to help at the store, but because she tended to be confrontational. The two fit together well. Although Sarah is pretty no-nonsense and doesn't back down from a fight, she's quite friendly once you get to know her. I tend to think of boxers like that as well.

In addition to Bongo, Shayla, a Himalayan, lived in the store. Shayla had lost her witch a few years back. She'd been young enough to get adopted again but hadn't matched with anyone except Sarah. Instead, she'd become a store cat, greeting everyone who came in and guarding the place when Sarah and Bongo went home.

Brian nodded at me and smiled. Sarah waved, and I waved back.

"So what was going on with Mason?" Natalie asked when I got to the table. Her mug held on the dregs of her tea.

Trinity had started picking at her scone. It was nearly gone so at least she'd started eating. Perhaps Mason's yowl had distracted her from her work problems.

"Mason felt someone's spirit. Not a happy spirit, either." I kept my voice down. We might not have many people in the café, but I didn't want to spread the news around too far.

"Like someone was killed?" Natalie said, her voice hushed. She might talk to everyone, frequently at a volume louder than she should, but she also knew the value of keeping her voice low in certain situations.

I nodded.

"Who?" Trinity asked, also whispering now. The way we were huddling, we were probably more suspicious than if we'd just talked normally. I noticed Brian glance our way more than once as I hurried to my place on the bench.

"I don't know," I said. "Mason thought he recognized the energy but didn't know who it was."

"So at least it's not your family." Natalie had clearly ascertained that would be my biggest fear and worry. All three of us were close to our families, though we might complain about them regularly.

Natalie's family was out of town, as was typical, so it's unlikely that they were in trouble, not given that a local police officer had gone off without getting his coffee moments before Mason saw the spirit. It takes a bit of time for spirits to orient themselves to wander and perhaps give warning to anyone with a sensitivity towards their death.

It wasn't normal for Mason to see spirits. Someone had clearly just died. They'd probably spent a few minutes hovering over their body, trying to make sense of what had happened. Upon realizing they were dead, the spirits can sometimes go fleeing around, attempting to contact someone they know. Disoriented as they are, they frequently get turned around and bump into any magical creature they happen to notice. In this case, it was Mason. Officer Alsez's call had to be about the same death. Waverton is neither that large nor that dangerous.

Trinity frowned. Her family lived in town, just around

the corner, not far from the cat café. The house Trinity had grown up in was just two blocks over, a big old two-story house built around the turn of the last century. It was brick with a narrow front stoop rather than a porch and a big old screen porch to the side where we'd spent a lot of time playing in the early summer and fall.

Her parents still lived there though Trinity and both her brothers had moved out. Trinity lived on the other side of town, about two miles from me, in a nice townhome apartment. Both of her brothers were attorneys and had their own homes in one of the older neighborhoods in town.

"I know Mason said he sort of knew them, but I didn't get the impression that he was aware of who exactly it was. He knows you far too well not to get a sense of your family," I told Trinity. She still looked worried. Her phone was out and her fingers flew over the keyboard as she texted her brothers and her parents.

There's this idea that magic and electronics don't mix. Waverton proves that untrue every single day. We use cell phones. I have a computerized cash register. My car runs just fine. People watch television through thunderstorms all the time and it's not a problem unless their house gets hit with a lightning bolt. Magic is the same way. Generally speaking, so long as I wasn't trying to put a spell on my computer I didn't have to worry about frying it. Except, you know, the same way anyone else would.

"Everyone has checked in," Trinity said. "My brother Tyson says that he's been seeing police activity around the library. He and Tim were worried about me."

Trinity had her eyebrows raised and she looked from me to Natalie.

"We need to check this out," Natalie said. She was already standing up.

Trinity looked back at her half-filled mug of chai.

"It's probably cold," Natalie said.

"It was supposed to be cold," I said. Only Natalie had chosen a hot drink on such a hot day. "I'll grab a paper cup and you can take it with you."

"We can't take the time..." Natalie started to say.

"I'll grab a cup," I said, already hurrying over to the coffee bar.

I'd had a carpenter rework the old dark wood bar so that there was a low area where the cash register sat and I'd pulled off the far end and put in a section with a glass front to show off the pastries. My espresso machine takes up a good portion of the employee side of the bar, the dark black of it rising up above the wood like a skyscraper. I love that thing.

I hurried behind the counter and grabbed a paper cup. No line of customers waited so I didn't feel guilty.

"What's going on?" Greg asked. He might have been young but he was reliable and available and willing to work pretty much full-time while he figured out what he wanted to do with his life. He wasn't the fastest worker but he was thorough

"I don't know," I said. "Trinity's brother said something is going on at the library." When people talked about the library in Waverton they meant the specialty library. When they meant the public library with ordinary books, they specified the word *public*.

"Wow. I wonder if that's why Officer Alsez left so quickly. He didn't even wait for his coffee," Greg said. No doubt to him this was a really big deal. I wasn't about to be the one to tell him about Mason's visitation. Even witches can get a little freaky about spirits.

"Hope you'll be okay for a few," I said.

Greg shrugged glancing over at Cade.

The café was uncommonly quiet. For the moment, the

only people in the café besides me and my friends were the people in the familiar room. I had another group scheduled to come in shortly. According to Natalie, the group was staying for a few days at the hotel and were looking at all sorts of familiars. I always hoped that one of my cats would make a connection and find the perfect home, but it's not always meant to be.

I quickly poured the rest of Trinity's chai into the paper cup and hurried to catch up with her and Natalie. Natalie was already out the door. Trinity was looking back giving me a hurry-up wave.

Like it had taken me any time at all. I handed her her drink. It wasn't even noon, but the heat hit me hard enough that I longed to head back inside to the air-conditioned space. I was thankful for my short sleeves, though they weren't much help with the humidity that seemed to press against my chest making breathing an Olympic sport.

Natalie marched along ahead of us. Several police cars were parked just off the street with their trunks hanging out into traffic. An officer directed drivers around. Another was on the far side of the library, but I couldn't tell what he was doing. No doubt they'd close the whole main street, which wasn't good for the café. I hoped my out-of-town witches could find the place.

Other people had come out of the buildings across from the library. I saw one of Tyson's paralegals on the sidewalk. Tyson wasn't there, but I had no doubt he'd hear everything he needed to when she went back in. He was probably busy enough that he couldn't stand outside watching. His paralegal probably didn't have the time, either, but if there was a crime in Waverton, Tyson and Tim might be pressed into service as attorneys and it made sense to have someone taking notes on what was going on in real-time.

The library itself was a large, eye-catching building with

three low concrete steps that ran the length of it, inviting people to run up them and go inside. The building had an unusual cream-colored façade that I don't know the name of, and between the windowed front and the concrete steps was a broad covered porch held up by off-white columns. Two sets of double doors led inside, the slight hair-tingling feeling of magic present when you reached them. The specialty library was another place that didn't attract the attention of non-magical folks.

It took a bit of magic to hide the five-story tall building. A basement hid below ground, though no one ever noticed that. Inside, the archives were on the top two floors and access was restricted. Not only were the archives locked behind doors, but more spells had been placed on those doors to keep anyone who wasn't supposed to be there out. Trinity was one of the few people, along with Eric, who had a key and had permission to be inside the archives. It was probably why Eric was so certain she'd stolen the book.

Of course, he could have taken it and was trying to frame Trinity. A really determined thief could have gotten past the security, too. Nothing is perfect, not even magical security.

A reed-thin, red-haired woman sat crying on the steps. Oddly, I didn't recognize her. A gray-haired, older woman was sitting with her, rubbing her hand against her back, slowly. Tom Alsez was with them.

An ambulance pulled up, sirens wailing. I had a very bad feeling.

3

"This looks bad," Natalie said. She tapped the toe of her sandal against the sidewalk where we stood. Her blue and white striped sundress fluttered around her legs as cars attempted to get past the library.

Having set up the barricade on one end of the block, Milton Janes, one of our oldest police officers, hurried down to set a barricade up at the far end. It would be easier to use magic but, unfortunately, we weren't supposed to do so where anyone could see. The red-haired woman and her companion were definitely outsiders, even if they were witches, which was not something I could ascertain from that far away. I didn't recognize the other officer who seemed to be directing traffic.

The smell of exhaust got stronger as the ambulance pushed its way through the traffic to the library. The siren was finally turned off so that I could hear more of the conversations around me. I hoped that someone knew something.

I waved at Jo from the herb shop down the way. She was a short woman who had a business specializing in organic herbs. She also grew some amazing cat grass and catnip. I'm not sure what she did to her plants but I found that Mason went wild for her catnip in a way he didn't for anything I planted for him, no matter what spells I put on them.

It wasn't just that they were organic. Jo had a way with plants.

While short, that didn't mean she was tiny. In fact, she was quite a large woman for her height. It didn't seem to make any difference to her. She was always running around taking care of her herbs and helping out others in town with their own gardens. She never seemed to tire.

I recognized most of the other faces on the street even if they weren't people I knew well. Peggy, who had the parrot familiar rescue, peeked her head out from the door of her rescue and looked worried. Her rescue was in one of the narrow shops right across the street from the library, rather smashed in between the bookstore and the bank. I wondered if Aloysius, her familiar, had said something to her about the spirit.

It appeared that all our police officers had been called out to assist in whatever was going on. That was definitely unusual. I completely understood why everyone was out and about. In a town like ours, sometimes magic gets out of hand and someone dies. It's a sad situation, but we're somewhat used to such happenings. It takes only one or two officers, medical personnel, and maybe a specialist in whatever magic went awry to take care of the problem. On rare occasions, the council might send a witch from the Witch's Bureau of Investigation to look into things.

This kind of response was not normal in any way, shape, or form.

"Everyone is out," Trinity said, almost as if reading my thoughts. With Trinity, it was certainly possible. She had a talent for picking up thoughts when the other person was particularly stressed. We were pressed close to each other, despite the heat, and knew each other well, too.

I couldn't back up to get any air between us because Brian Welks was now behind me looking out at the street.

"This looks bad," he said.

I couldn't disagree, although I'd have loved a bit more space around me. It seemed like everyone who had been in the area had wandered out to see what was going on. Given the traffic being directed, a few had come from further away. I imagined the rumors going around on the magical grapevine.

A gasp rose up from around me when the coroner's van pulled up. Elaine Winters is our coroner. Her brother Blue runs the funeral home. Blue had a knack for seeing spirits and I wondered if Elaine was out on an official call or if the spirit that Mason encountered had finally found Blue and let him know something about what had happened.

Elaine's a large woman, taller than a lot of men and quite broad, though I've seen her dressed up to the nines and her figure is to die for. Her frizzy gray hair takes up as much space around her head as she does in a room. For all that she works with bodies on a regular basis, she's one of the funniest people and everyone in Waverton enjoys having her at a party.

"Someone had to have died," someone whispered. It sounded male but I wasn't sure who it was, only that it wasn't Brian.

"Murdered, I'd say," someone else whispered back.

I heard the vague sounds of whispers from further away, though the words didn't reach me. Everyone had an opinion.

The ambulance left, no lights or siren. I looked at Trinity and Natalie. They were both listening to the whispered speculation behind us as well.

The sun beat down on our heads. Sweat had broken out

along my neck, and my armpits were dripping. I wished I had something to fan myself with. Even better, I'd have loved something to drink. With all the people around, I worried that folks would start fainting without something.

"Keep an eye out here," I told Trinity, longing for her iced chai. "I have to go back to the shop. It's hot out here and people might think to come in and get something to drink."

The cafe carried bottled water for those who didn't want coffee or tea. I also had some flavored waters, though they weren't real popular around our town. Magic could flavor water easily and most locals grabbed the plain stuff when they wanted water. Occasionally, ordinary people visiting from out of town would purchase one. Fortunately, flavored water had a long shelf-life.

I pushed my way through the crowds. People let me through, some with the presence of mind to say hello. When I crossed the side street between my café and the block the library was on, the crowds dropped to almost nothing. Just a few people pausing to look at what was happening.

I hurried inside, breathing a sigh of relief after the heat.

"We need to put more water into the coolers," I told Greg. He and Cade and I were alone in the building. The women visiting the cats had finished their time and left. I wondered if they'd joined the crowd in front of the library or if they'd hurried off to their car hoping to avoid a traffic jam.

I went into the familiar room to clean up anything they might have left behind and scoop the litter boxes. I had spells to keep the litter box odor down, but even magic can only do so much to mask the smell of a fresh deposit.

I gave Mason a quick ear rub. He was back on his high shelf watching everything. One of the other cats, a beautiful long-furred two-year-old black beauty named Kitika put a paw on my wrist and purred a bit. I spent another moment with her before checking on the others.

"Have our next guests called?" I asked when I came out. Normally, I stayed pretty booked up. Even the witches in town, those that had cats or other familiars, sometimes treated themselves to an hour with my cats, petting them and loving on them. I know the familiars appreciated the extra attention and it was good for many of the witches, particularly those who hadn't chosen a feline.

Greg shook his head. "Weird, huh? Do you suppose they have anything to do with what's happening outside?"

He'd clearly been pacing around the café, looking out when he could. The tables were all spotless and organized perfectly. The ones nearest the window closest to the library were still damp as if he'd been wiping them down just recently. I couldn't blame him.

"I did see a couple of people on the library steps. She was crying. I didn't recognize her, so she could be our out-of-town guest. I should have asked Natalie."

"I'll bet she'll respond to a text," Greg said.

Natalie was known for her ability to respond to texts practically before they were sent. It was probably a low-level psychic attunement though Natalie denied it. She believed a quick response was just good customer service. I tended to think it was probably a bit of both. While it might be interesting to test my theory and see if she could respond to a text I didn't send, I was far too curious to wait.

I pulled out my phone and sent her a quick note.

Moments later, hardly enough time for her to have felt the buzz in her pocket—Natalie always has her phone on silent—much less to have tapped in a response, I got a text from her.

The woman on the steps wasn't your visitor. That's an older witch with green and gray-streaked hair and two friends who are equally elderly.

I frowned. I looked up to see a woman with gray hair

streaked with green just coming through the door followed by two companions

"I'm so sorry," she said. Her voice was surprisingly light, though she walked a bit slowly. "We had such a hard time finding parking. What a mess out there. Do you know what's going on?"

"I don't," I said. "It looks like someone was injured or perhaps even died." I wasn't sure I wanted to engage in gossip, but I also didn't want her to think the town was always this way.

She gestured to the taller woman with a short graying bob that framed her face beautifully. A stooped, older woman stood next to the tall woman, hanging on her arm for support. "Clara said we'd run into some trouble coming here this weekend."

"Mrs. Ainsley?" Greg said.

Mentally, I thanked him for having a name. In all of this, I'd forgotten to look it up.

"Can I get you and your companions something to drink? Jade can bring you into the room and I'll bring the drinks right on in if you like. We seem to have a slow moment."

Greg was definitely earning his money just then. Thankfully. I glanced back and noticed the waters were all out in their place. Good.

"I'll have a cool water," Mrs. Ainsley said.

"I'd love an iced latte," the tall woman said.

"The same for me," her shorter companion said. I wasn't clear which woman Mrs. Ainsley had been pointing to when she named someone Clara.

Greg and I got the three women settled in the other room with the cats, while Cade went in back and started putting water in the refrigerator back there.

In the familiar room, Mason did his duty making sure all

of our familiars were around to see if they were interested in Mrs. Ainsley as a new companion.

I wasn't surprised that Kitika had made herself at home on Mrs. Ainsley's lap and didn't look at all interested in leaving. She had been pining for her own person practically since she'd come to me. She was a young cat and apparently hadn't been terribly bonded to the witch she'd lost.

Shortly after that, other people started wandering into the café. As expected, they were mostly getting water. A few got iced coffees or a chai. None ordered anything too fancy. While we always got a flurry of people just before lunch, those that wanted a quick pick up rather than a meal, I had a feeling this was the start of the rush of people who'd been standing outside in the sun.

Trinity hurried in, her eyes shining with tears.

"What is it?" I hissed from my place making coffees.

Trinity glanced around like she didn't want to say something in front of the line of people in the café. It seemed like that was always the way. I'd had a more than quiet morning and just when things got busy, a friend needed me.

I pulled Trinity behind the counter and gave her a quick hug.

"What?" I whispered.

Trinity made a small sign. I felt the spell going over us. She really didn't want anyone to hear this.

"It's Eric," she hissed. "He's the one dead." Then she began to cry.

"That's horrible," I said. Although, really, it seemed rather like karma fulfilled. He'd been a horrible man. No doubt he'd mistreated the wrong person.

Trinity nodded. "The police asked me to come in for questioning later. They'd have done it now, but Tyson's assistant saw they were talking to me and made sure he was there. I have to go to the station and give an official statement. They said, before they let me go, that I shouldn't leave town."

I felt Trinity shudder in my arms. I knew she worried they'd think she was a suspect. But if everyone Eric was angry with was a suspect, so was the entire town. And then some.

I couldn't help Trinity other than to offer some comfort. I made sure she had a quiet place to recover herself. She refused anything to drink, though I forced some water on her. She had been out in the heat for a bit. Chai, even iced, isn't nearly as hydrating as water. I got her settled at our usual table in the back, thankful Cade and Greg had been so intent upon cleaning everything.

I learned the specialty library was closed until the police finished their search. Several of the witches in line for drinks had felt Trinity's little spell. They continued to look curiously at us, wondering what we were discussing even as I got her settled at a table.

Fortunately, most people were local and knew all of us. Clay Bridges took his coffee over and sat with Trinity for a bit, just talking to her. Clay runs the feed store a few blocks over. It was definitely a major event for him to get out of his store and grab something. He's the kind of older man who likes his coffee hot and black no matter the weather. I suspect he'd love it if I made it so strong you could stand up a spoon, though he's assured me mine is okay as it is. Just okay is not what a shopkeeper wants to hear.

He and the Lyons family have been friends for years. Clay might live out on a farm a few miles from town but he had made a point of being active in his younger years and had even sat on the town council at one point. Now, his store took all his attention, but he remained popular in town, and, if you knew him well enough and asked nicely, he could give you the low down on almost any thread of gossip.

I worked hard pulling drinks. Cade made sure Greg had backup when he needed it at the register but kept the back area clean while grabbing supplies from storage. People grabbed bottled water from him before he could even put a case of it in the cooler. I'd have to order some extra the next day or I'd run out.

I did a small spell to make sure I remembered before going back to pulling drinks.

The crowd dissipated around the time Mrs. Ainsley and her companions finished their allotted time. The small trio wandered slowly out of the room when Cade let them know their time was up.

"That Kitika is such a lovely girl. I have her on my short-list of potential familiars," Mrs. Ainsley said. She smiled sweetly at me, waiting to hear my opinion.

While I was pleased, I had a niggling sensation that something wasn't quite right. She seemed like such a sweet older woman and Kitika needed someone to dote on her, but I had a tight feeling in my gut.

"Well, we'll see how things work out. You mentioned having other places to visit?"

Mrs. Ainsley was only too happy to tell me more than I wanted to know about her visiting schedule, which sounded absurdly busy. She and her friends were looking at the parrot rescue, the goat rescue, and even the horse familiar breeders.

The latter surprised me. Horses took a lot of work and few people were willing to let just anyone care for them.

I greeted the next group while Cade went to pull drinks. Six non-magical people, three guys and three girls. The two tallest of the guys were holding hands. Two girls, one of which looked like one of the guys, were giggling together. The final couple was a young man and a girl. Probably college students off for the summer and looking around for something to do. So long as they abided by the rules of cat café, I was fine with it.

I headed into the cat room to straighten things up and make sure the cats had everything they needed. Magic tingled around me. I wondered if it lingered from Mrs. Ainsley and her crew. The people who had just come in hadn't indicated an interest in a familiar and when they'd registered online, I hadn't gotten any hints of magic.

"I think they're non-magical," I told Mason.

Kitika had no desire to bond with an ordinary person so it was unlikely that she'd come out of her house, though she'd been loving on Mrs. Ainsley.

Jelliane didn't like that old woman at all, Mason told me, speaking of Mrs. Ainsley. *She's certain there's some negative energy around her. I'm not sure how she was so certain when Kitika thinks she's fine.*

"Could it be ill-health?" I asked. I didn't know Jelliane well enough to know how accurate her impressions were.

Mason paused, thinking. He clearly hadn't had a good hit. The door behind me opened before he could give me an answer.

Greg normally doesn't allow anyone in until I'm done clearing. Drawing my hand away from Mason like a guilty child, I turned.

It was the girl with the boyfriend. They were both in shorts and sandals. They had their drinks, expensive specialty frozen coffee drinks. Her dark hair swirled messily around her shoulders.

The girl was pointing at Kitika who was hiding in her favorite little cubby.

"The cats will come out for you if you sit down," I said. Greg and Cade were busy with the rest of the drinks, making more fancy things, so perhaps they didn't understand that they were supposed to wait.

The girl didn't even look. She continued walking towards Kitika, reaching in to touch her.

I heard Kitika hiss.

"I said that you need to wait until the cats come out to you." I put my hands on my hips. All the felines were racing to their perches, out of reach. Kitika was huddling back in the little house.

The girl turned to look at me. "What do you know?" Such attitude. I was sorry I'd let these people in.

"I know because I'm the owner. If you can't follow the rules, then you'll have to leave."

"I spent my money. We can do what we want." The girl stood up, drawing herself up like she was spoiling for a fight.

"No. Actually, you can't. There are rules here." I wasn't worried about her. A quick spell and she wouldn't touch anything. However, her attitude riled me.

"Don't talk to my girlfriend like that!" the guy was also drawing himself up. It would have been funny in another situation. I'm maybe five-three and he was barely an inch taller than I was. He had the beginnings of a beard, but it was so thin you didn't notice it until you were up close. Unfortunately, I stood far too close to him.

I gestured with my hand putting a protection spell on myself and all the cats.

"Last warning," I said. "You can sit down and let the cats come to you or you can leave." Not that any of the cats would be foolish enough to spend any time with these two. There had to be a way to pre-screen the ordinary folks who came into the café.

The girl rolled her eyes and copied my quick gesture. I felt a hint of magic surge around her, magic flowing easily, but unfocused, so no protection spell was created. From the amount of magic around her, it wasn't that she didn't have the power. Most likely she had no idea what the gesture was supposed to do. Great. An untrained witch.

First, someone is murdered in the town and then I meet a teenage witch with more attitude than training.

5

The girl and I had a stand-off. She stared at me, daring me to say something more. Technically, because she hadn't actually cast a spell, she'd not broken any rules. I took in her dark eyes, trying to read what she knew. Oddly, I thought maybe I saw fear there. She felt the magic though I doubted she understood what it was, not given the anxiety in her eyes. It made me wonder how much the attitude covered the terror of what she was now noticing.

Most witches were raised in witch families. Some came to their magic later in life, though usually, that meant at puberty. This girl was beyond that age. As powerful as she was, I found it hard to believe she'd not been noticed and reported to the council so she could get training.

"Hey guys," the two boys came in. They weren't holding hands now. Each had a fancy drink. I mentally racked up the expense and the money they'd spent already.

"This place sucks. Why did you want to come here?" the girl asked.

"What's wrong?" The boy, or perhaps young man, was slightly darker-haired than his partner. Both had shoulder-length dark locks and clean-shaven faces. Both were equally tall and thin and wore khaki shorts that fell practically to their knees and fancy short-sleeved pullovers.

"She won't let me pet the cat I wanted to pet," the girl said.

"Flori," the talkative guy said. "Not everyone will put up with your crap. And cats don't like being forced."

When Flori had stood up, Kitika had made a beeline for one of the higher shelves, cuddling up with Mason. I noted his muscles were tense and ready to take on anyone who tried to harm the other cat. Jelliane was cuddled behind the tiny little Siamese Alcari. Not a surprise. Alcari had an attitude problem. Half the reason she was around was to learn to put up with humans. She was probably gloating at the bad behavior.

Flori flounced over to the chair that Mrs. Ainsley had just vacated. I thought I saw a puff of dark smoke come out. Smoke like that signified serious negative energy. I hadn't had a chance to clear the room so I had no idea if it was left over from the previous visitors or if it came from Flori herself. No matter her attitude, I found it hard to believe the young woman held onto that much negative energy. She was too busy throwing it around at other people.

"So what's up?" the other two young women came in. One looked at Flori and the other looked at the young man with her.

"Flori is having a hissy fit," the dark-haired spokesman said.

The two girls looked at each other and settled in on chairs as far from the one Flori was in as they could. "I told you," one whispered to the other.

I suspected that most people wouldn't hear her but I'd done a protection spell and that includes being able to hear what your enemies are doing. While the girls weren't my enemies, they were in the room and I'd done an inclusive spell.

Great. Even the girls weren't thrilled with Flori. I was going to have to monitor the group. I went over to the far side of the cat café area. There's a little cleaning closet that allows me to clean litter boxes at any time. Beyond is a hallway to the backdoor that I use in the evening. The stairs to my second-floor apartment were just outside so it was easy to come and go.

I slipped through the nearly hidden closet door and knelt down to pull boxes one at a time and clean them out. I was closer to the cats if they needed me, but I wouldn't be bothering the group as much as if I'd stayed in the room.

I kept a careful ear on Flori and the young men. The cats weren't feeling friendly and none came down.

Towards the end of their visit, when Flori was complaining loudly, Alcari came down and settled on the lap of the most outspoken of the guys. Flori started to stand up but I saw a wave of force push her back in her chair. I'd have to speak to Mason about Alcari's use of force. At least she didn't go all ninja cat on her.

Flori looked perplexed at what was going on but, uncharacteristically, she said nothing. When their time was up, she stood and complained at what a waste of time it was. Alcari leaped from the young man's lap and went up to one of the perches.

The other cats watched, still huddled on the back of the shelves. I noted positions and muscle tension had lessened from what they had been earlier. They were more relaxed now that Flori's visit was ending.

I came out in time to escort them out. Flori held one of the pillows with the face of a Siamese cat on it. I stood by the door and indicated that she couldn't leave with it.

She glared at me, throwing it behind her before flouncing

out with her friends. I needed to say something to the council about her. She was a disaster just waiting to happen. Actually, she was probably beyond help with her attitude, but you never knew. Not my decision.

Unless she wanted one of my familiars. She wouldn't be getting one. I'd be sure to let the other breeders know, too. That reminded me, I hadn't given Tom Alsez the information about when Mason heard the spirit.

"You good for a few more minutes?" I asked Greg.

Greg nodded. While it had picked up after the murder, we didn't normally do as much business in the afternoon. Cade worked until four when Charlene came in. Greg worked until closing with Charlene, though she stayed a bit later to make sure the cats were taken care of.

Opening the door, I felt the oven that was the afternoon sunshine. I would be so glad when the heatwave was over. I drew in a deep breath, or as deep as I could against the heat, and started down the road to talk to Officer Alsez about what Mason saw.

6

Someone had decided long ago that the police station didn't need to be on the main street where my café sat. Instead, they placed it a few blocks behind my building, near the courthouse and City Hall. Instead of parallel parking, the buildings had a small parking lot, and street parking was angled, something I could have wished for in the main shopping district. Parallel parking and I do not get along.

I walked down towards the station on a narrow brick covered street that ran beside the café. I smelled BBQ from the restaurant on the far corner. It's a cute little place with some of the best BBQ I've ever had, though the owner swears it's because it's Louisiana BBQ. I don't care where it's from. It's good.

I passed the little movie theater. Mostly it ran third-run movies so people in town could get a night out. The high school often had special nights to make a bit of money selling their own popcorn. Waverton residents were very supportive.

The theater also showed movies about working with

familiars and the occasional underground documentary about witch and human relations. Witches, of course, were human. It's just that witches had a bit of something extra that allowed the use of magic.

Certain humans have appeared to learn how to do magic, while others seemed unable to do so. No one has isolated whether the ones who could learn were genetically different than those who couldn't. Researchers tried using both magical methods and scientific DNA inquiry to figure it out.

At the corner, by the BBQ place, I crossed the street and turned left. This street was wider, more like the one my café was on. The regular library was located across the street from the BBQ place, which I had to think made working close to mealtimes tough. I certainly couldn't have worked smelling the wafting scent of their great BBQ while my stomach growled.

The library was right next to the courthouse, which was a large Federalist-style building in old, blackened bricks. I loved the columns and the wide, rounded porch leading up to it. A drive led up to the courthouse on the side opposite the library and ran around the back to a parking area. Waverton Park sat beyond the parking area.

The park wasn't great for children as there was no play equipment. Basically, it was a big grassy area with a few trees. Mostly it served as a space for official city festivals to be held. The park ran behind the courthouse and its neighbors for four blocks before it was bisected by streets. Driving, you could tell it was only a long block wide, but when walking, it seemed wider, probably because whenever I cut through there I was walking at an angle.

When the town was young and even smaller than it was now, I'm sure the founders thought the park was a great, central space to meet. Lots of witches hate leaving their familiars behind, not that witches with horses and cows have much choice. In those days, though, perhaps cows and horses would have been welcome.

Nowadays, it's different. Wandering around with a cow would make you eccentric at best. A town full of people with cows and horses and cats and dogs would be remarked upon. So, despite a perfect place to gather with our familiars, it's mostly just witches who come to gatherings. Even dog familiars are required to have a leash, though everyone knows no good familiar would run away.

As I walked through the park, I noticed a few people sitting under the trees reading. I wiped a bit of sweat from my brow, not certain how they could concentrate. A couple of folks walked their dogs on the trails that ran around the edge of the green space. I have to admit that I felt more like the dogs with their tongues hanging out than the people walking. Did they not feel the heat?

Finally, I passed City Hall, ready to cross the street to the police department. The police station had recently been moved to this newer building, all sharp angles and mirrored, tempered glass. While I didn't dislike the general look, I didn't like the way it combined with the older buildings in town, three of which had been demolished to make room for it.

That had been a huge controversy when it happened. Personally, I preferred the look of the old buildings but understood that they had so many structural issues that they couldn't be saved. We didn't have a lot of choice as we'd already voted for a larger police force which required more space than we had had in the basement of City Hall. Still, I wished they'd gone with a look that blended in with the rest of the stately old buildings, something boringly rectangular and brick, maybe with a few columns.

The station was set far enough back from the street that there was a small parking area in front. Another, larger lot surrounded by chain-link fencing sat behind the building and was for official police vehicles. I crossed the blacktop, hot enough to make the soles of my feet warm even through my shoes, and hurried up the two concrete steps in the front.

Mirrored windows lined the front, with wood posts between. Around the side, where there were fewer windows, the outside was lined with whitewashed brick. The doors, surprisingly, were solid wood, though up close I could see through the windows on either side of the doors into the lobby where an officer waited to assist people through the metal detector.

I knew that Jonas Fikus, who often manned the entry, was particularly good at spotting witches and had a nose for who was thinking about trouble. At least that was how he described it. Considering that there was rarely trouble in town and this was often credited to Fikus, it was too bad you couldn't bottle his talent and sell it to the TSA or Homeland Security.

White tile that would last forever lined the entry foyer. I knew there were spells to make it easier to clean and to keep it from absorbing magical energy. Fikus sat at his usual post. He was a short but round man, and it was clear that he knew how to fight. Anyone who did any fighting regularly would recognize the broken nose. He wore a black uniform and although the entry was pleasantly cool, the wood stool he sat on was in an area that picked up a bit of sun and he had sweat along his hairline.

"Afternoon Miz Jade," he said.

"Afternoon." I gave him a smile and a wave while I put my purse on the conveyor belt.

It went through just fine and Jonas waved me through the metal detector. Once cleared, I followed the blue arrows to the main part of the station.

I chatted a bit with Lani Thomas who had been assigned

to the front desk. She'd been a year ahead of me in school and had always been scholarly. Everyone expected that she'd go into law, but as an attorney, not a police officer. After a year of school in Lexington, she'd come back saying she had no desire to spend any more time among stupid humans. She'd joined the police force. Although she was required to go through the academy outside of town, her time away was far shorter than if she'd gone through all the years of university schooling a law degree required.

Lani took me back to talk to Brendon Spader, the police chief. He was taking charge of the investigation himself. I didn't know Brendon that well. He wasn't from Waverton and had only been chief for a few years. He lived just outside the city limits on two acres and his wife raised goats. She spun the wool into yarn which she hand-dyed and made goat's milk soap that she sold at craft fairs. I heard she did very well.

Gossip said she magically infused her soaps for relaxation, energy, or concentration depending upon the scent she gave it. While she did not specifically spell her yarn, other witches knew she kept it pure enough for the most delicate spell work. Some non-magical folks purchased the yarn at the fairs, but, mostly, they went for her soaps. Witches kept her in the yarn business, typically through online ordering.

Brendan's office was towards the end of the long hallway, facing the front. When Brendan told us to enter, I noted the large window with blinds that kept the room shaded. File cabinets, two tall ones and then two lower ones in between to form a sort of credenza, lined the wall to the left. Brenden's desk was large enough for work but not so big that it was a showpiece, merely a pressboard-style thing that gave him a place to set the computer and work.

I sat in one of the uncomfortable-looking upholstered, light wood chairs across from the desk, surprised to find they weren't nearly as bad as they looked, not that I planned to spend any time sitting. The room stank of burnt coffee, something I can't stand working in the business I do. I hoped that my interview with him would be short.

I sat on the edge of the seat just to be sure that he noticed that I wasn't exactly getting comfortable.

"How can I help you?" Brenden asked. I should probably think of him as Chief Spader, but most people were on a first name basis in Waverton.

"Officer Alsez was in the familiar café when he was called to the specialty library. At least he got a call and left and shortly after that, we noticed things going on at the specialty library," I corrected.

Brenden nodded, his bald head shining slightly in a bit of sunlight that snuck through the blinds. He had his arms resting lightly on his very clean desk. I have a desk in the back of the café and it's never as clear as his. I had heard there was plenty of paperwork in policing but perhaps they'd gone all digital.

"Just after he left, my familiar, Mason, howled from the feline room. I went in to see what had happened. We had some non-magical people in there so I was worried. The humans were fine, and none of the cats appeared in trouble, except for Mason, howling. He's not normally like that, particularly not around ordinary folks," I was babbling, I knew. I reminded myself to stop it.

"When I reached up to touch Mason, he immediately let me know that he'd been in the presence of a disturbed spirit. Someone had just died, probably violently."

Brenden looked interested in that.

"I thought that the police should know in case that helps with the timeline," I said. I didn't add that I knew they were talking to Trinity because she worked with Eric and I didn't want her in trouble.

"Did your familiar know who the spirit belonged to?" Brenden asked.

I wondered if there had been another murder around the same time. I spent half a moment debating whether to ask that question or answer and then ask.

"He said the spirit was familiar but not someone he knew well," I said.

"I'm sure by now you know that Eric Boyd is dead. Had your familiar ever have a chance to meet him?" Brenden asked.

Mason would have known of Eric, though he wouldn't have actually known him personally. Eric came into the café from time to time, but he'd never really spent time with the cats. Still, Mason knew Trinity quite well and he'd have sensed Eric's energy on her.

"No. I mean, not in any real capacity though they might have encountered each other. Eric does…I mean did come to the café for coffee now and then. He wasn't a regular. Mason is always in the feline room during my work hours." I hoped that all made sense. Anyone growing up in Waverton would know that familiars could get a sense of people even through glass, particularly if their witch was interacting with them. However, the familiar wouldn't necessarily know them well enough to identify if they hadn't spent time with the person directly.

Brendon nodded and pulled out a keyboard and made a note.

"Was someone else killed?" I asked.

"Hmm?" Brenden looked back at me.

"You asked me if Mason knew who the spirit belonged to. Like, I don't know, maybe someone else had died at the same time?" I felt silly pressing the issue but if someone else had died the town had a right to know.

Brenden pressed his lips into a thin line. "Frenchie Rolf

was killed by Eric's familiar goat Jojo at about the same time. It was likely an accident from when Jojo felt Eric's passing, but I needed to make certain."

"That's horrible," I said.

Frenchie wasn't exactly anyone's favorite person. He had a tendency to sneer when others would smile. He also tended to say exactly what he thought without a care for the feelings of another person. Not in a cute way but in a way that suggested his cruelty was calculated as to how much he thought he could get away with.

He'd call fat people fat and do so as if he were just making an observation. It was a rather passive meanness.

He was an older guy and retired, but he made a few extra bucks doing a bit of daycare for needy familiars. Jojo was more than a handful even at the best of times and our local familiar sitter, Whitney, had recently refused to look after him while Eric was at work.

So, Frenchie took over.

It wasn't unheard of for familiars to act out—cats scratching and hissing, dogs biting, at anyone who came close—upon the death of their witch. Horses and goats, even cows, might kick and head-butt and run around crazily until they came to terms with the initial shock of grief.

"Frenchie's never come into the café," I said. "Mason's never had reason to run into him that I know of, not with me there. It seems like it was probably Eric he sensed."

Brendon nodded and made another note.

He thanked me for coming in and let Lani lead me back down the hall to the entrance. I'd done my duty, even if it didn't feel like it had been nearly enough. Particularly not when I was leaving and saw Trinity's brother Tyson pacing around outside, his cell phone to his ear.

7

Tyson gave me a sudden and unexpected smile when he saw me, the arm not holding the phone quickly going up in a wave. He ended the call and walked over to where I stood.

"What's up?" I hated that he didn't look quite as over-heated as I felt. So much warmth burned in my cheeks that they had to be bright pink, and while he had a slight line of sweat still dotting the edge between his dark hair and his brow, the shirt he wore wasn't sticking to his back quite as tightly as mine.

I have to admit that Tyson had been my first crush. I mean he was tall, well-built, and had nearly perfect molded-clay features. His eyes were deep brown, almost black, and when he smiled he always looked pleased to see you. After he finished law school and joined the family firm, his fashion sense became impeccable with finely tailor suits in colors that always flattered.

"They're holding Trinity, pending charges," he said, clearly frustrated. He stepped off the curb and then back on, not paying attention to anything but his gloomy thoughts.

"That's absurd. I was just in the station telling Chief Spader that Mason saw a spirit just after Officer Alsez got a call," I said. "Trinity was at the café then."

"Trinity said that in her interview. I thought they'd at least come talk to you. There was the usual discussion about how well familiars can distinguish spirits if they didn't know the person well. Someone argued that it could have been Frenchie, who was no doubt as horrified to have died as Eric, no matter that his death was ruled an accident. No matter that we have a familiar acting out, the coroner still has to give an exact time of death, just in case any non-magical people end up involved."

"Elaine's good," I said.

"I know." Tyson kicked at the curb with the bottom of his foot. I smelled the musky scent of his sweat and thought how much I liked it. Too bad he'd never seen me as anything other than a friend of his little sister.

"But it could take some time for her to write up her report because it'll require a cause as well," I finished.

Tyson nodded. "Unfortunately for Trinity, there were patrons in the library who heard Eric go off on her this morning about a book missing from the archives, more than just the kid who thinks he saw her kill Eric."

"She mentioned the book when we had coffee this morning. Trinity, Natalie, and I had been talking for maybe half an hour before Officer Alsez got the call. She'd have been working before that and usually mans the front desk…"

"Eric sent her off to do some shelving," Tyson said. "So that meant she wasn't at the desk and no one saw her shelving, naturally. I mean it's normal. People aren't looking for the library worker putting books back on the shelves."

Shelving would have been a slight demotion from working the front desk. Normally, the part-time workers did that. Trinity hadn't mentioned her morning demotion in duties. Of course, if Eric had lived, it probably wouldn't have lasted. Trinity was a good worker and everyone loved seeing her at the desk.

"I'm surprised that Eric was willing to raise his voice in public," I said. Whenever Trinity had talked about him getting mad at her he had always berated her behind closed doors.

"I'm not sure he knew anyone was around. An out-of-town witch heard him yelling and she heard the name Trinity," Tyson said. "It's not an actual accusation and it says a lot about Trinity that she was willing to own up to the fact that her working relationship with Eric wasn't exactly easy."

"The whole town knows that, though. I mean half the town wouldn't even apply for a job there because no one wants to work with him. In fact, I'd say that more people in town had reason to murder him than didn't." No one liked Eric, really. It was sad that he was gone and particularly upsetting that Trinity might be getting blamed for it, but he wasn't a nice person. And he wasn't popular.

"That's the issue," Tyson said. "With so many suspects the police are going to have a heck of a time narrowing it down. I was just on the phone with a PI that our office works with and she'll be coming out to look into what happened. I'm not taking any chances on my sister."

"I wouldn't either," I said.

Tyson looked up and down the street and sighed. "I guess that's about all I can do here. Trinity has given me all the pertinent information."

"I wish I had gotten to the station earlier today to let them know what Mason saw. I think if I had said something earlier..." I broke off as Tyson shook his head.

"It wouldn't have mattered given your relationship with Trinity. Fortunately, we can get a familiar communicator to come in and relay Mason's message. It can go back channels if it comes to a trial with non-magicals involved."

He was right. Tyson and I stepped off the curb together and crossed the street back towards our offices. I pulled at my shirt a bit to try and create a bit of air to cool off. Really hot days like this are not the norm. We were towards the end of a heatwave. I was actually a little surprised that there hadn't been more crime during it.

Thunderstorms were forecast for the evening. Rain was even forecast for tomorrow. Even if it didn't materialize, maybe some clouds would keep the temperature down to merely hot.

Tyson noticed the movement. "I will be really glad when this weather breaks. I've had so many calls about petty crimes lately."

"I can imagine. People always seem to be on edge when it's as hot as it's been."

"I've had more than my usual out-of-town calls, too. Not all of them witches, which surprises me. I guess our name is getting around."

"Good for you guys," I said. And I meant it. Tyson and his brother Tim—someone liked the letter T—were good attorneys. They deserved to have good fortune.

"It makes it harder to defend Trinity," Tyson said. "I know this is weird. I don't get premonitions. Mom does a bit, but she's had no feelings one way or another about this, but I feel like this extra work is all a distraction. Very strange."

"There've been a lot of outsiders at the familiar café, too. People that surprise me they're coming." I relayed the story of Flori and her friends and what a problem they were. "I haven't talked to Natalie about whether the hotel is busy or not, though."

"It *is* summer so I'm sure the hotel is busy. It always is," Tyson said. "And cat cafes are popping up everywhere.

Maybe people from around the area want to see what the fuss is about."

"I got the impression the kids today were students. Maybe they were home on break. I just think Lexington is an awful long drive to see a cat café. Plus, I heard there was one in Georgetown now. That's way closer." Naturally, I'd assumed that the kids were from the University of Kentucky up in Lexington. It wasn't an impossible drive, perhaps an hour if they lived on the south end of the city, but Georgetown was definitely closer and a far easier drive.

Tyson shrugged. He might feel like he was being distracted, but clearly, his premonition didn't extend to the whole town. Interesting. Still, now that he'd mentioned it, it felt like something was going on. I would have to talk to Mason after I cleaned up the feline room and fed the café cats.

8

I felt guilty for leaving work early. Charlene normally gets the familiars settled for the evening. Mason gets to snooze in the familiar room until I come and get him after work or when I pack up to leave. I do a lot of paperwork at home and sometimes I'd go up and start working on the books and Mason might have to wait an hour or so until I get him.

That evening, I took care of the cats. It gave me a chance to be sure none of them appeared upset about Flori. It took me longer to settle the cats than it did Charlene and she had locked up and gone home before I was finished. I tended to spend a bit more time obsessively making sure all the cats were in good health and not upset about anything that happened during the day. I talked to Mason about everyone, as I typically do. He's always willing to give up details about the cats' day.

Once done, I had to persuade Mason to get in the cat carrier. He is not a fan of the carrier. Mostly I let him walk outside and up the stairs but with the heat I worried about his paws getting burnt.

Naturally, he was displeased about the indignity, thinking I should have just picked him up and carried him from the door to the stairs. I'd have needed an extra arm to do it his way given that I had my purse, my laptop bag, and some paperwork from the café that I planned to work on after hours. My social life is currently limited, hence the brief fantasy about Tyson. Rather than dwelling on my crush, which wouldn't come to anything, I figured it would be more productive to focus on my business.

I walked up the outside stairs to the landing in front of my door. When I felt generous, I called the area a little balcony. Once inside, the apartment opened up into something amazing with a large open great room with a living area, eating area, and an island kitchen. I had no doubt that from the shape of things, that the kitchen had once been a narrow galley kitchen. At some point in the recent past, the apartment had been remodeled and opened up and could now be a model for one-bedroom living.

A fireplace made of brick from the original building was the focal point of the living area. Another brick chimney went through the bedroom. I had no idea if that brick was from a fireplace that had once been downstairs or if there'd been a fireplace in the bedroom, or perhaps if it had even serviced a second little apartment.

Beyond the great room, I had a powder room that opened onto the hallway. A larger bathroom which included a big rounded bathtub and shower combination was off the bedroom, along with a walk-in closet. There was the largest linen closet I had ever seen next to the powder room. I had two closets near the entry as well. My mom was jealous of the storage in this little place, and I had to admit it was impressive.

I loved working in my kitchen. Mason had his own food in a dish near the island and was chowing away while I put on some noodles and started mixing up a sauce. I was going for a garlicky butter sauce and I'd add some mild sausage, shrimp, spinach, and carrots to go with it.

I paused when I noted Mason was slowing down on his food. I used a quick spell to amplify my connection to him so I didn't have to be touching him to chat.

"Tyson had a premonition that a lot of his busy-ness was a distraction from something going to happen in town. Have you felt anything like that? We have been busy at the café." I turned the heat down on the water just a bit. I didn't want it boiling too quickly. The sauce needed to be nearly done first.

Mason raised a paw to wash his face. He paused a moment to savor something he'd found caught on a whisker and then went back to washing his face. It was soothing to watch his white paws with the pink pads moving quickly over his ginger and white face.

We've been busy with a lot of outsiders. I'm not sure how outsiders would make a difference, though, Mason said.

"Could they have been spelled to decide to come here, now?" I asked. Flori didn't seem like she'd be easy to spell, but her friends might be. They'd probably be susceptible to anything she did accidentally which might make them easier prey for someone else.

Possible, but what's the point? Mason asked.

"No one in town liked Eric. If we didn't have a lot of visitors, then the police would look more closely at people in town. With others around, maybe they won't." I threw the sausage into a frying pan to cook that up first. I also added a bit of onion. I should have purchased mushrooms, but it was too late now.

You said they were looking at Trinity. She lives in town. If that was the plan, it didn't work very well. Mason went on to wash his creamy white chest.

"Well, it does make it harder for Tyson to focus on her

case. Maybe someone hates Trinity and they're setting her up," I said.

Mason paused and looked at me. His eyes were brilliant green, which was what made me ultimately fall in love with him. *Then why have all the other people in town?*

"Maybe as a back-up plan, in case their set-up of Trinity didn't work?" I suggested. I wasn't a criminal mastermind so I didn't have a clue what I was doing.

Seems thin, Mason said. And I haven't had any premonitions about busy-ness in town or otherwise. It seems normal to me. Except for that Flori, who is definitely a powerful untrained witch and needs to be reported.

"I already sent an email to the council," I said.

The council wasn't someone you contacted any other way. They had an email form you used to check off boxes about what the problem was. Different departments had different areas, including problems with other witches, suspicion of negative magics, and untrained witches. The council liked their mystery. They did everything they could to keep ordinary witches from knowing much about them, other than the WBI division, which they made sure had a visible presence in the magical community.

"You said Mrs. Ainsley had negative energy. Do you think she's just sick or do you think something else is going on?" I asked him, remembering that.

Jelliane noticed, not me, so I couldn't say. Flori, however, was bad news, Mason said. Or she could be if she knew how to use her powers. She seemed like a brat, but I'm not sure she's all bad. Not yet.

"Opinions on Mrs. Ainsley," I asked draining off the fat from the sausage. Next, I'd cook the shrimp and spinach which went fast. I turned the water back up and got the noodles ready to toss in.

I tend to think her negative energy may be because she's not really the nice person she wants people to believe she is, Mason said. He went back to pulling at one of his toes.

I nodded. "Do you think Kitika would be okay going with her?" If Mason said no, then it was a no. Mrs. Ainsley could complain all she wanted but everyone would back me up. We didn't adopt familiars if we didn't think they'd be safe. There were other places to find a familiar. I hoped, suddenly, that she'd end up falling in love with someone else. Kitika deserved someone nice.

Jelliane isn't much given to suggesting someone isn't nice. She's suspicious but mostly keeps that to herself. I think there are better options for Kitika. Besides, Mrs. Ainsley is old. Kitika has already lost one witch, Mason said.

The last part was as good an excuse as any for not adopting her to Mrs. Ainsley if she did come back to see about an adoption.

I finished making dinner and was just sitting down to eat when my phone rang. I looked at the number. Natalie.

It was a little strange that she'd just call and not text. "What's up?" I asked.

"Trinity has been officially arrested. They said someone saw her kill Eric!" Natalie was practically in tears.

"What?" I couldn't quite wrap my mind around it. I was thinking of spells that would make someone look like Trinity. I also thought about all the people in town, ordinary folks who might not understand what they were seeing. Maybe there was something to Tyson's premonition. Maybe it went to him because it involved his sister. Of course, then her mom should have noticed it, too. I wondered if he was just stressed out by the success of the business.

"There's this red-haired witch named Fiona McIvers, can you imagine, registered here even! She was the woman crying on the steps earlier as if she'd known Eric. I've never seen her name in the register before this."

Knowing Natalie, she'd looked. Probably used a spell to make sure she didn't miss the name. Better than a computer search any day because a computer could be modified, or a name misspelled, but magic would have shown her what she was looking for even if someone erased it. Of course, if someone were really good with a certain type of spell, they could fool Natalie's magic, but that would take planning and talent.

"She said she saw Trinity?" I asked.

"No. There's a boy with her, probably her son. I didn't see him. He said he saw Trinity," Natalie said. "And as a result, Trinity has been arrested. I just heard the gossip, but no one has called me."

"Or me," I said. "I went in and told them about Mason seeing a spirit. Trinity couldn't have done it."

"We know that," Natalie said. "So we need to make sure the police do."

"I'm not sure what else I'm supposed to do. I know Mason will talk with a familiar communicator about his experience," I said.

"The police have decided on a perpetrator," Natalie said, talking as if she actually knew anything about law enforcement. "We need to give them the real one."

"I think Tyson said he was calling in an investigator from out of town," I said. Probably a witch.

"Deborah Canton," Natalie supplied. "She's been in town before and I just got a reservation from her company. I'm not sure how good she is. I think she just likes spending time with Tyson. Rumor has it, he likes spending time with her, too, if you know what I mean."

My heart sank. The one person I had to hope cleared my best friend was probably dating the man I had a crush on. I told myself to suck it up. This wasn't about me. It was about Trinity.

"No matter why she's here, she has to be good otherwise the Lyons wouldn't use her services for their company. I mean, if Tyson likes her, he can just ask her out."

Natalie made an annoyingly non-comital sound. "I wouldn't count on it." And with that, she clicked off.

9

I spent the rest of the evening thinking about everything going on. Natalie seemed to think that Deborah wouldn't actually help Trinity. I couldn't imagine that Tyson would be so blinded by an infatuation that he'd risk his sister's freedom, especially when there was no way Trinity could have murdered her boss.

First, she was with me and Natalie when Mason learned about Eric. It was even possible that Eric wasn't quite dead when the police were called. I had no idea how he was killed or what had happened, but dying slowly gives a different feel to a spirit and Mason had been shocked and a bit frightened about seeing one. So while Eric might have lingered, he didn't linger long.

Second, Trinity wasn't a killer. She was the one who wouldn't take biology in high school because you had to dissect things and she couldn't do that. She can't stand the sight of blood, either. Trinity fainted when Natalie fell and cracked the side of her head. Blood had leaked everywhere and even I'd freaked a bit. I did manage to get an emergency stop bleeding spell on her so we could call someone. Later, I learned that while head wounds bleed a lot, Natalie's life hadn't actually been in danger from the blood loss. She'd been in more danger from potential trauma to her brain.

If Eric's killer had used poison, I suppose it was possible Trinity had murdered him, just, but unlikely. Trinity was a great believer in putting out what you want to get back. It's why she tended to be an upbeat person and softer spoken than Natalie—or me, to be honest.

So, even if the timing worked, I couldn't believe that Trinity did it. Of course, Eric's spirit wouldn't have been able to tell Mason anything about his murder. He probably hadn't even fully processed that he was dead yet, which was why he was floating around and ended up in the café.

Finally, I didn't see the motive. Trinity wouldn't have killed Eric over potentially being fired. There were so many complaints about him from so many people, that had she gone to the board, there was a good chance that they would have backed her rather than Eric.

The only reason the police were looking so closely at Trinity was that the boy claimed he'd seen her kill Eric. I wanted to know what he'd actually seen. Perhaps he'd seen a woman with dark hair. Or seen Trinity talking to Eric and later decided she was killing him. I realized as I sat thinking that I had far too many questions.

I walked over to the bookshelves that lined part of the living area and opened the lower doors. Mason raised his head from where he was napping on the sofa to see what I was getting into.

He loves to lie on the deep green and blue afghan my mom had crocheted for me. She's spelled it with soothing calm for when I'd get anxious about my business. Mason had taken it over. He swears he's reinfusing it with further calm, but I think he's drinking up my mom's spell. Still, it's not like the magic dissipates by use, just over time.

I have a thing for journals and notebooks and I tend to pick them up wherever I go. The one I chose for this particular list was spiral bound with a picture of a Siamese cat lying on a sandy beach. It had the word Savannah on it and came from my trip to Savannah Georgia. Like all witches, my must-visit places were New Orleans, Savannah, and Salem, though the latter had been more of a pilgrimage.

I settled on one of the stools at the kitchen island and started writing down my notes. When I finished with what I'd outlined, I tapped the pen against my chin, thinking. Eric's murder and Trinity being accused of murdering him weren't the only things going on. I worried I'd forget something. Mentally, I started going down my list of concerns.

If Mrs. Ainsley wanted Kitika, I was going to need to deal with her. I also needed to warn the other familiar adoption centers about Jelliane's impression of Mrs. Ainsley. It was only an impression, but they should know. Some familiars can stand up to the pressure of negative magic, others are already on the way down the path, but a few are good souls that wouldn't understand why they were doing something wrong. Those needed to be protected from someone walking in the shadows.

I turned a page and made notes of who I needed to contact about Mrs. Ainsley.

I turned another page and started to think of suspects for Eric's murder. Pretty much everyone was a suspect. I could reasonably rule out Greg, Cade, myself, Natalie, and Trinity because we'd been together in the café. I thought back to who else had been there. Brian Welks, Tom Alsez, and Sarah Meyerson were in the café around the same time, though I think Sarah had left by the time Mason saw the spirit.

Still, it wouldn't have given her much time to kill him, though Sarah had as much reason as anyone to kill Eric.

Always having to be an expert, Eric often suggested that

Sarah didn't know what she was doing when it came to books. He claimed that there were many volumes on magic and familiars easily available, but that she refused to carry them. He actively sent people out of Waverton to order books through a specialty bookseller in Louisville rather than ask Sarah.

Most locals knew what he said wasn't true, but the people coming from out of town didn't always know that, which lost Sarah business. She continued to run her bookshop and seemed to do well enough, but I had no idea how much Eric's comments hurt her bottom line.

The only reason the police wouldn't be looking closely at her was that she'd been in the café when she would have had to be in the library to kill Eric. If the police insisted that Trinity could have done it, then so could Sarah. In fact, it would have been easier for Sarah than for Trinity.

I would hate to point fingers at an innocent person but I didn't want to see Trinity going to prison for something she didn't do. Bad enough that she had been arrested.

Mason yawned and leaped down from his bed and wandered over to twine around the legs of the stool and rub against my toes.

If I had known that Trinity would get arrested for this, I would have tried to stop the spirit rather than sending him on, Mason said. He sounded rather apologetic.

"Not your fault," I said. "Given the timing, I'd love to know when the boy thinks he saw Trinity. And what she was doing. I just don't have enough information."

Mason closed his eyes. Familiars who are friendly with each other can communicate telepathically. It's not something that they can do just generally. It requires a certain amount of permission. I had once equated it to giving out a phone number but Mason says it's a bit more personal than that.

I can choose to ignore a phone call. He can't ignore a tele-pathic communication.

I talked to Dodi Purr, Mason said. Dodi Purr was Lani Thomas' familiar and had spent time in the café before bonding with her. He'd been a young cat and I'd only had him in the café because the breeder hadn't been able to place him. He'd been very shy and retiring. Working with Mason and the other familiars he'd come out of his shell.

Lani had been looking for a familiar around that time. She might be a police officer, but she walks softly and normally moves with the grace of a ballet dancer. She doesn't often make sudden moves, perhaps having learned that sudden moves may exacerbate a tense situation, though I suspect it's just her way, which made Dodi Purr feel more comfortable.

He's heard that Eric was hit over the head. If he wasn't killed instantly, he would have died soon after. Lani was not privy to the interview with the young man, Isaac, who claims to have seen Trinity. However, he described Trinity very clearly, Mason said.

Interesting. Dodi Purr would have more impressions that he had gotten from Lani, but for whatever reason either he or Mason had not chosen to share them with me. Sometimes it's a matter of not wanting to give out too much personal information about an owner. As Lani and I weren't close, I was grateful for that. After all, Dodi Purr would likely let her know about the conversation since it pertained to her work life.

I sighed, wondering where else I could dig up information.

I'd start by talking to Natalie and see who's staying at the hotel. But that's just me, Mason said. He slipped away from the chair and sauntered down to the bedroom, probably a hint that it was getting late and I should at least try and get some sleep before I had to open the café in the morning.

10

The morning came far too early. While my café mainly showcased familiar domestic cats and found homes for them, it still served coffee, which people want bright and early in the morning. I was opening, which meant Mason and I had to be there at five so I could make sure that everything was set. I had to double-check that everything had been well cleaned the night before, get the espresso machine up and running, and, of course, clean out kennels and litterboxes and make sure the eight cats I had in the café had plenty of food.

I didn't open as early as some folks would like largely because I'm not much of a morning person. Anyone who really needed a caffeine fix before I got there could use the drive-thru coffee place at the edge of town. They opened an hour before I did.

While I complain that I'm not a morning person, what I really mean is that I'm not an "it's so early it's still night" kind of person. Getting to work at five means I have to be up at four-thirty and I can get up that late thanks to living upstairs.

If my alarm ever stopped working, Mason would be sure to wake me. Heaven forbid he miss a meal.

Despite hating getting up, I liked the way the world felt when I finally pulled myself out of bed and got outside. It was always quiet. On that morning the air had yet to heat up, though I knew it would. The parking lot was wet, and in the early morning light, I noted the clouds hovering over us. It was less humid than the day before, but I wasn't sure if the promise of breezier air would hold up. I disliked the stillness. The afternoon could be uncomfortable. I could also be pleasantly surprised by a thunderstorm, not that thunderstorms are always pleasantly surprising. Just when it's ridiculously hot.

My mother had a natural weather sense, but I didn't inherit it. If I wanted to know the weather, I had to do a spell. Mason was better than I was, but his weather sense was more about barometric pressure, which, he informed me, was dropping. With any luck, we'd get more rain. I kept my fingers crossed.

I heard a few cars out on the main road. The day smelled clean as if last night's brief thunderstorm had washed away the sweat and fears of the crowds the day before. I wished that helping Trinity would be so easy.

The familiars in their kennels all started meowing the moment I opened the door. Mason was silent. I knew that he knew what was going on without a single meow, but they all mrrped and mewed for my benefit, hoping to hurry me along. If meows were ever directly translated to words, this particular tone would be "Hurry! Hurry!"

No one was injured. Everyone still had some dry food, which I called crunchies. I made sure all the cats had access to crunchies at all times. They might not be the most nutritious food, but they were safe to leave out so that no one would ever get too hungry. The cats got canned food once in the evening. It appeared that everyone had eaten heartily as not a single dish had a scrap left.

When I opened the kennel doors, they all eagerly leaped out and hurried through the little cat door to the main area to claim their favorite spots. They'd be after me to refill the bowl out there soon enough. After all, cats, even familiars, do not want to eat stale crunchies.

I made note of litter box habits and wrote all that in a notebook I kept. I had adapted the one I'd seen in the shelter. The notes allowed me to keep a closer eye on how the cats were doing and track any worrisome symptoms or behaviors.

Once the kennels were cleaned and the cats had more food, I washed up and got to work on the front. I had the timing down to a science.

Mitsy Luther came in just as I opened the door. She works at City Hall and is almost always the first one in the cafe. Every once in a while she's my second customer instead of my first. There's a coffee shop closer to City Hall, but she says it's too crowded in the mornings.

I was finishing up with her mocha latte when Reggie Witherspoon came in. Reggie lives just around the corner and works out at the horse farm where the horse familiars are bred.

"I heard about Trinity," Reggie said, keeping his voice down. Reggie knows my father quite well. They grew up in Waverton together. He was one of my first customers and he's made it a habit to stop on his way to work every morning.

"It's so frustrating," I said, not bothering to whisper. No one was in the room to hear us. Mitsy was already out the door. "She was here when the spirit came through. Mason saw it and he yowled at me. A familiar communicator will be able to verify that."

"Chief Spader is a good guy," Reggie said. "I'm sure that it will all work out. And Tyson and Tim are the best lawyers in town so she's well-represented. I heard their investigator got here yesterday, too."

Reggie's familiar wasn't a horse as you'd expect, but a crow. My dad said that Reggie's first familiar was an older horse who had lost their witch and then bonded with Reggie. Dad suspects that Reggie was still too torn up when that horse died to bond with another horse. Instead, he'd bonded with the crow.

I suspected there was more to it. Reggie and the crow fit. Like crows, he loved to know things. I suspected that the bird fed him most of the information Reggie put out there, hoping to get the real story. I didn't care how he found things out, if it helped me learn something, I wanted to hear it.

"I hope you're right," I said. "I mean I went and told the chief what Mason knew and that Trinity was here so she couldn't have done it. It's just that I heard there was a witness who said they saw her."

"Heard it was messy," Reggie said quietly. "Bludgeoning. Eric was way too big for a girl like Trinity to take on."

Trinity wasn't a tiny girl and she was stronger than Reggie gave her credit for, but I wasn't going to stand there and argue. The thing was, bludgeoning was messy and bloody and I couldn't imagine Trinity ever beating someone, even a single blow to the head as Dodi Purr had implied in the discussion with Mason. Even if she did, her clothing hadn't been the least bit mussed nor was her hair or face. She looked ordinary, even breaking a light sweat by the time she got to the cafe.

I knew there were spells people used to clean up spills but it seemed like blood spatter would require more magic than the average spill. Trinity would have had to magically clean her whole person. Magic takes energy. A spell like that takes a lot of energy. Trinity didn't act as if she were overly fatigued when we talked. That I would have noticed.

"She couldn't be in two places at once," I said. "And I know her well enough to know she was here."

Reggie nodded at me and patted my hand. I was saved from having to say anything else by Tom Alsez who was coming in for coffee. This was early for his morning coffee.

"Early for you, isn't it?" I asked when he got up to the register.

"Actually wanted to chat with you about the timing of Trinity Lyons visit yesterday morning," he said. "Chief said that although he had to arrest her because of the witness, he's not convinced she did it. Too many people saw her here with you and Natalie."

"I'm glad to hear it," I said.

"Chief is getting pressure to solve the case *now*, and that the powers that be like Trinity for it," Tom said quietly. "You keep that to yourself except for maybe if you happen to see one of her brothers."

I just stared at him, not certain what he was trying to say. The powers that be probably meant the mayor, but for the life of me, I couldn't understand why the mayor would want Trinity convicted of a crime. It's not like I knew the mayor well or anything. I mean, not more than I knew anyone in Waverton.

"I normally take my break about nine-thirty but once a week Trinity and Natalie come in and we chat, about ten-thirty. Natalie is always late so Trinity and I just expect to meet at ten-forty-five or so but we don't tell Natalie. Then we talk for maybe half an hour, sometimes longer. We were close to finishing our morning when everything happened."

"How did Trinity seem?" Tom asked. He made a note in a book.

"Fine. A little bit less hungry than usual. She was upset

about the accusations Eric had made about her stealing a book. She hadn't taken it, but they can't seem to locate it."

Tom nodded. "We had a call there early in the morning. Before all this, from Mr. Boyd. He filled out a complaint about a stolen archival book. Pointed his finger at Trinity."

"She said she didn't do it," I said. "And it would be unlike Trinity to just misplace it."

"Boyd said he did locator spells and it wasn't in the library. It was gone. He said it would fetch a good amount on the dark market."

"Trinity wouldn't even know how to go about doing something like that," I said. "You have to know people. Trinity doesn't."

Tom made a note. "All consistent with her statements."

Well, that was good. I was glad I was helpful with something.

"We've got a familiar communicator who will be in town to take Mason's statement later this afternoon if you're available?" Tom looked up at me.

"We can be. Greg is good about covering, but if it's after four, I'll have someone else working."

"We'll make it later then," Tom said. He gave me a nod and left without even purchasing a coffee.

11

I fumed over the information I got from Tom for the rest of the day, which ended up being busy. The clouds kept the day cooler which meant more people were out and about. Plus, everyone wanted to gossip about Trinity's arrest.

They say that there's nothing like a small-town grapevine. Add in magical familiars with telepathic abilities, and in Waverton news travels at approximately the speed of light. I hated that Trinity was the focus of the mess.

It seemed like everyone in town came into the café and wanted to hear what I thought about one of my best friends being arrested. I avoided talking to people as much as I could. Fortunately, the crowds allowed me to avoid answering as many questions as I might have had to if it had been a quieter day.

The crowds, unfortunately, kept me from running off and hiding in the back cleaning litterboxes. Greg was my only other employee that morning and there were far too many people to just leave him alone in the shop. Greg is a good solid worker, but he's not the faster barista in town.

I let Greg take care of the appointments for the café and getting people settled with the cats. I took money and made drinks because it kept me running so people couldn't expect me to stand around answering their questions. I probably could have talked more even so, but I didn't want to. Instead, I listened to the conversations that people had while they waited in line.

I learned that Fiona and Isaac were visiting from Arizona. Those who had encountered them tended not to like Isaac. Apparently, he'd had a tantrum at Ned's Diner over his breakfast. The eggs were scrambled too hard. Instead of asking nicely, he'd thrown a fit. Fiona and the older woman with her hadn't helped at all. They'd let him scream and curse at the waitress when she brought out his order.

The second time the eggs weren't scrambled hard enough and he'd thrown the plate at the waitress. Fiona said nothing.

I heard David Cullins who ran the diner came out from the kitchen, comped the food they'd eaten, and then made them leave. Apparently, he'd told them in no uncertain terms that they weren't welcome there any longer.

The gossip speculated that the older woman was Fiona's mother but no one really knew for certain.

Fiona, Isaac, and the woman who might or might not be her mother had gone to Shirley's bakery, where I get my scones, and had gotten a muffin. Isaac had complained about the muffin being stale. Fortunately, they'd not returned to complain to Shirley. That would have been an argument to see. Shirley had a temper. When she got mad, she had a tendency to throw spells.

Everyone agreed that Fiona spent a great deal of time crying over every little thing.

Rumor had it the group was there for a familiar. Isaac wanted an iguana, but none of the iguanas over at Chet's had liked him. From what I was hearing, I was unsurprised.

Lizards are very astute observers of human behavior and they tend to either completely approve or completely disapprove.

Other rumors suggested the Fiona was looking for assistance with a sick bird familiar, but those weren't nearly as interesting as the thoughts about Isaac. It didn't stop me from paying attention, though. Trinity was my friend and I intended to get to the bottom of what was going on.

Everyone said they knew someone who knew someone at the police station last night when the group had made quite a scene. Apparently, Fiona thought that Chief Spader wasn't taking Issac seriously when he didn't immediately call for Trinity's arrest. The chief had attempted to explain that Trinity had an alibi, but Fiona refused to hear him. Instead, she accused him of calling her son a liar.

Suddenly, the mayor's pressure to have Trinity arrested made sense. The mayor had people in her town putting up quite a fuss.

People lowered their voices when they talked about what Isaac said. I'd had to listen particularly hard and almost missed out on hearing anything because the gossips kept waiting until I started the espresso machine. Still, I had all day, and eventually, I caught on that Isaac had insisted that everyone at the café must have been lying.

Fiona was a bit more politic suggesting that Trinity had set this up to make us think she was somewhere else. All in all, listening to the gossip about the family, I was starting to think Fiona might have been the murderer. It would certainly explain her behavior and the behavior of her son.

I pulled another latte, letting the milk heat in the machine. The line of people had gotten shorter as the day wore on. I suspected that everyone who wanted to ask me questions had come in. Now that lunch approached, they wanted more than just coffee.

By that time I was working by rote and was quite surprised when the name I called belonged to Tyson.

"Busy?" he asked quietly.

"You could say that," I said. "I didn't even realize it was you. I've been keeping my head down. Everyone wants to know what I think."

"Downside of a small town. If you have a tragedy everyone wants to be able to say they talked to you about it," Tyson said.

"I heard your investigator was already here." I needed to get back to work, but I'd been on the machine without a break except to run the cash register while Greg got the cat visitors settled. I needed to pause, if just for a quick chat.

Greg, perhaps noticing, picked up a few cups and made sure there wasn't anything he could quickly make or get started.

Feeling guilty, I moved back to the machine and started on the next drink while I chatted with Tyson.

"She is. Right now she's looking into the eyewitness. I guess his family isn't the most reliable," Tyson said.

I wondered if she'd then look at me and at Natalie. I wondered how reliable she'd find us. I mean Natalie had always been Natalie, which meant pushing boundaries and getting her own way. I'd been a bit lost until I founded the café. I'd worked in the familiar shelter but while everyone praised how good I was with the cats and dogs, I'd been written up more than once for saying something I shouldn't to a potential adopter.

The shelter itself wasn't very big. It wasn't like there are tons of witches letting go of their familiars. Sometimes a familiar will get disgusted with the use of negative magic. Cats, especially, can get ticked, and, as Jelliane had proved, a feline could sense when someone was pushing the boundaries of positive magic.

Since I started the café, the current shelter mostly took in dogs. They still had some space for cats, but they tended to keep the cats that were the most socialized and most likely to be placed quickly. I had the others here at the café where they could spend time with people, even if the people weren't all witches.

"Given that I was nearly unemployed before the café, how reliable am I?" I asked.

Tyson gave me a smile and shook his head. "It wasn't just you here with Trinity. It was Natalie and a handful of others, including Officer Alsez."

The fact that Tom Alsez was a police officer was going to go a long way to getting Trinity off the hook.

"I don't even know how Eric was killed," I said, hoping to draw Tyson out. I mean, I'd heard the gossip and Mason told me what Dodi Purr knew. Tyson would undoubtedly have more details. Unfortunately, he looked around at the line, short though it was, and shook his head.

I waved as he left, quickly picking up the next drink and calling out a name.

When noon rolled around I sent Greg to lunch and did my best to keep up with the line of people. It had slowed down, but the hour he was gone felt long considering how hard we'd worked. The good thing was that the tip jar was plenty full so he'd be well compensated. I leave tips to the employees. I figured as the owner, I got paid better and had other perks.

By the time Greg returned from lunch, the line was gone and we were down to our usual afternoon lull. I was restocking the cooler and taking inventory of what we were out of.

"That was some morning," Greg said, putting his apron back on.

"It was," I said, looking up. "And I'm now starving. I ought to check in with Mason before I grab lunch, though."

Greg nodded and got to work cleaning up behind the counter. I'd kept it as tidy as possible but it needed a good scrub. Doing a bit more now would make it easier when we did our final clean-up.

I slipped into the cat section of the café. Two young men and two older women were in separate sitting areas. Jelliane was with one of the younger men rubbing her chin against his hand. That was good to see.

I reached up to give Mason a chin rub.

About time, he said leaning his head out.

"Anything in here?" I asked.

Gossip, he said. Most of what he'd heard was similar to what I'd heard about Isaac and Fiona. However, he had more details about Chet. I guess Isaac had insisted he was bonded with one of the iguanas and had pitched a fit when Chet told him no.

Given what I've heard, I'm surprised he didn't try to insist Chet killed Eric, Mason said.

That was interesting. I wanted to know why this young man was so focused on Trinity. So far as I knew, she hadn't been to Arizona and if the gossip was to be believed, that's where Isaac and Fiona were from. It seemed like the most important thing would be to learn why they wanted to set her up for a crime she didn't commit.

I spent the rest of my day wondering why Isaac's family would want to frame Trinity. From what I'd heard, I tended to think that Fiona had murdered Eric and she and Isaac felt like it would be easy to pin the crime on Trinity. I briefly considered whether I thought Isaac could do it but decided that at around eight years old, maybe ten if he were small and immature, he wasn't strong enough to have bludgeoned a man to death.

Still, small towns love their theories when they gossip. I'd heard about any number of people, including Sarah Meyerson at the bookstore, who had reason to want Eric dead. Unfortunately, I'd learned nothing about why Isaac might be so focused on Trinity.

After the café was closed, I called Natalie.

"Well?" she asked, without even greeting me on the phone.

I was still down in the café, sitting on my favorite club chair with Mason lying on the rounded arm beside me. He was eager for dinner but he knew I was distracted. He kept glancing at the kennels where he no doubt smelled the aroma of canned cat food. I heard the cats at their dishes eating heartily.

"I just got done with work," I said. "And decided to give you a call about what I heard."

"I've been hearing things here. Like that kid, Isaac, who is certain Trinity did it. Can you believe they came in here and started talking about it and wanted me to agree that it had to be her?" Natalie said.

"What did you say?"

"I told them that I was one of the people with Trinity and if they thought I didn't know my best friend, then they were idiots and ought to find a new hotel." I heard Natalie fuming.

"Did they?" It would have served them right to have to find another place to stay. The closest hotel to town, if you weren't at Nat's was forty minutes away.

"They said they would but didn't check out. They still haven't. They're probably searching online for a room somewhere else. I was pretty booked as it was, and with the murder, we've had some bloggers along with experts show up and I couldn't accommodate all of them. I bet that the closer hotels and B&Bs are all filled."

"If Fiona and Isaac don't leave, at least we can investigate them," I said.

"I heard they're from Arizona," Natalie said. As if that told us anything at all about them. Lots of people were from Arizona. Some of them were even witches. Most of them weren't lying about people in our little town.

"I was wondering why they focused on Trinity," I said.

Natalie was silent for long enough that I started to get uncomfortable. I don't mind silence in a conversation, but on the phone, I like to know the person hasn't just set the phone down and left, leaving me listening to empty air for however long I want to waste my time. It goes back to a bad experience in my teen years.

"I don't know," Natalie finally said. "It is interesting, isn't it?"

"It's like they have a personal grudge against her. Did you ever know if Trinity went to Arizona?"

"Not hardly," Natalie said. "She's not a traveler. Remember how hard it was to get to come to New Orleans with us?"

I did remember. Trinity liked being at home, in Waverton. She'd worried about her familiar, her brothers, her mother, and father as if all of them weren't adults.

"Could she have met Fiona or Isaac while they were here?" I asked.

"We ought to show her a photo," Natalie said.

"If we can see her."

"Bail," Nat replied confidently.

"I hadn't heard that she got it." Which was a huge surprise given the number of people in the café gossiping all morning.

"I have to go to the station to have Mason interviewed," I said. "I should get going."

"Find out about bail. I just assumed..." Natalie said trailing off. So perhaps Trinity didn't get bail after all.

I got Mason's carrier and put him inside, which he grumbled about. I promised him treats for waiting patiently. Then I headed out the door to go to the police station with my cat so that he could be officially interviewed.

Waverton is the rare place where that can happen. I wondered what any ordinary folks would think if they knew I was taking my cat in as a witness to murder.

When I got there, we were escorted to a nice room where the familiar communicator waited. She was dressed in a flowery skirt that reached below her knees. Her shirt was a short-sleeved blouse that was the opposite of flowery, but somehow it worked for her. Her black hair was bundled back in a ponytail with curls spilling in a waterfall around her shoulders.

She sat on a blue loveseat in front of a scratched wood coffee table. A single end table sat beside her. Across the way was another loveseat, the wear more obvious as no one was sitting on it. The color of that one was uneven and I suspected that it was a hand-me-down.

The cushions were thin in parts and less thin in others.

The coffee table was almost as scratched as the loveseat was worn. I noticed a large dog bed for canine familiars to relax on in the corner across from the end table. The place smelled of animal musk but otherwise wasn't bad, probably better than the human interview rooms. Familiars didn't just pee where they wanted.

I felt badly for the familiar communicator having to spend much of her day in the room with its walls a plain gray unbroken by a single window. Chances were, if there were horses or goats to interview, then she hadn't spent the whole time in the room. Large animals were interviewed on site. I suppose I could have demanded she come to me to interview Mason, but the station wasn't far, and Mason tends to be agreeable and confident no matter where he is.

"Sorry I'm late," I said. It had taken longer than I expected to walk to the police station. I guess carrying an eleven-pound cat slows me down some. By the time I had reached the place, I was regretting not having driven, but driving had seemed foolish when I'd left the café.

"I was running behind anyway," the communicator said. "I'm Alice."

I shook her hand. Once the door was closed, we let Mason out of his carrier. He leaped onto the coffee table and looked at her.

Alice leaned forward, not touching him but looking into his eyes with a disconcerting seriousness. I wasn't sure how

Mason felt, but I wouldn't want to be looked at like that. I'd be afraid that someone was going to tell me something horrible. My mind searched around for what, but I had no frame of reference for anything that bad.

Mason sat looking at her. They sat that way for perhaps five minutes which stretched interminably for me. I had nothing to do but didn't feel as if I could pull out my phone and start texting. No magazines sat anywhere around to give me something to look at. I didn't want to fidget too much because I didn't want to distract Mason.

According to the rules, I had to be in the room to verify that Mason was my familiar. However, I couldn't touch my familiar during the session. At one point Mason's fur raised slightly and I had to sit on my fingers to keep from petting him to try and comfort him.

After the longest five minutes in the history of mankind, Alice leaned back and smiled.

"Thank you for bringing him in," she said, looking at me. "He's a fine cat."

Mason was already walking into his carrier.

"Are you allowed to tell me what he said?" I asked.

Alice nodded and pulled out a book that had been in the little drawer of the end table. "I spell this book to take down our conversation in writing. It needs to be written down. We've yet to come up with a spell that records thoughts so that people can hear, unfortunately."

I took the book from her. Magic wafted from it. Whoever had set the spell, whether Alice or someone she worked with, was powerful. The book opened to the page about Mason, listed as Mason Owlens, which always makes me laugh when the vet gives him my last name. Alice had described him before letting him speak. Of course, rather than using the term ginger, she said "red and white bicolor" which sounded so clinical.

Mason had basically told her what he'd said to me. In the time since he'd become more certain that it was the spirit of someone he had met. Upon seeing images, he picked out Eric but not with any certainty. He did know, though, that the spirit didn't belong to Frenchie.

I nodded and gave the book back.

"Is that pretty much what he told you?" Alice asked. She was back in super serious mode. I wondered if she had a spell to make her look at if she were about to tell you were sentenced to die. Because that's what it felt like to have that serious look turned on me.

"Except for the fact that I didn't question him about who it was. Only that the spirit was familiar, like someone he'd met before."

"He doesn't really recall meeting Eric," Alice said. It was probably her job to poke holes in our story.

"Eric has been in the café. I'm not sure Mason has met him directly. I'm fairly certain that when I opened, Eric socialized with the cats in the cat room."

Eric, being Eric, had insisted upon giving me advice on the care and feeding of feline familiars. He acted as if I couldn't be trusted to know that sort of thing, no matter that I had studied to be a vet tech and worked in the shelter for several years. I'd been nicer to him than I should have because he came back about a week later and started criticizing my setup and telling me how it should have been done. While his ideas weren't unheard of, I'd talked to the shelter and other cat café owners to find out what had worked best and his suggestions hadn't made the cut.

While I'd tried to be nice, I remained firm in my choices and held my ground. He hadn't returned after that.

Alice nodded. "So recognizable but not known," she said.

"Exactly. I don't think Frenchie ever came in. Maybe once to get coffee, but definitely less than Eric. I also know Eric better than Frenchie, too." When touching, Mason and I communicated telepathically. My understanding was familiars picked up impressions about people their witch knew, too.

Alice's book made a few notes based on our discussion. She closed it again and put it away.

"Thank you both for your time," she said, standing. She was shorter than I had expected, perhaps half a head shorter than I was and I'm not all that tall.

We shook hands and I loaded Mason up to return home. All the while I continued to wonder about why Trinity had been chosen. I really needed to talk to her.

13

Mason was hungry and grouchy enough to paw at the edge of the carrier so I didn't stop at the front desk to ask about seeing Trinity. Instead, I walked back to my apartment. It really had been foolish to carry him all that way. It wasn't so much that he was heavy. Instead, the carrier with him in it was awkward and unbalanced. Mason, being a cat, had to move and turn to see what he wanted to see. I was constantly compensating for his movements.

Fortunately, the low clouds had kept the day to a dull warmth. It was humid, but not like it had been, and for that, I was grateful. By the time I got home, I was only lightly sweating. First things first. I fed Mason. I badly needed a shower, so I took a quick one of those.

I was hungry, too. So, after showering, I called Natalie to see about dinner.

"I'm on the late shift," she said, "so I can't. I don't know what I was thinking. Not that I usually go out on a Wednesday."

When we finished our quick chat, with no further discussion of Trinity, I picked my purse and went out to the deli and got something quick and easy to eat. Irene's deli is a standalone place right next to the grocery store. I know a lot of grocers have delis inside now, but Irene's had been in that spot long before delis inside a grocery were common. While I could purchase sliced meats at the store, if I wanted a decent sandwich I went to Irene's.

She offered a wide variety of meats and cheeses and items to put on your sandwich. You pick the bread, which meat and fixings, and the sandwich was made right in front of you. Sandwiches could be hot or cold. Personally, I thought the pastrami was to die for.

As usual, when I entered, the store smelled of rich, roasted meats and the tang of pickles. Soft music played in the background so that you didn't hear my shoes squeak on the black and white tiled floor as I walked to the counter to fill out my order form. A few tables sat on either side of the main aisle, all of them white square four-tops. The chairs were neatly pushed in and the tops were wiped. The deli was well on its way to closing.

I decided on pastrami on rye with Havarti, onions, and a bit of mustard and mayo. I had a pickle on the side, though I didn't like them on my sandwich. I also treated myself to chips.

Mark Gander was working the counter. He was a few years ahead of me in school and had to take special classes. He'd grown from a quiet, shy boy into a sweet man, if a little quieter than normal. He'd adopted a beautiful gray tabby as his familiar. I'd seen him at the pet shop many times shopping for her.

"How are you, Jade?" he asked. He didn't make eye contact with me. Instead, he worked on my sandwich. He'd already pulled the card that I'd filled out with what I wanted.

I noted that it was slow in the deli, but they were only open for another half an hour.

Lyn Wells, the current owner was in the back starting to clean things up. She'd waved at me but let Mark start the order. Mark rarely handled money so I knew she'd be out shortly.

"A bit stressed with everything," I said.

"I heard about Trinity," Mark said. "I'm sorry. I don't think she did it. Trinity isn't the sort of person to hurt anyone. She was always nice to me in school."

Being a bit slow and definitely not what people call neurotypical, Mark was often the butt of cruel jokes at school. Trinity had always been one to stand up for him. I could say Nat and I also did, but if Trinity weren't around, we were far less likely to get in the middle of something that we felt wasn't our business.

I'd like to say I got better as I aged, but I really didn't, though I had always liked Mark.

"She was with me when it happened, I think," I said. "Mason saw a spirit that he kind of recognized while Trinity, Natalie, and I were having coffee yesterday."

Mark nodded. "She'll be okay then because she has plenty of people who saw her somewhere else."

"For some reason, a boy named Isaac decided it was Trinity he saw in the library and he's making a big deal out of it, or his mother is," I said.

Lyn came out, washing her hands. Mark handed her the paper while he wrapped the sandwich. He added a pickled in its own wrapping.

"That brat was in here today," Lyn said. "Mark was nice to him, but I was ready to come to blows. I have no idea what he has against Trinity."

"I wish I could talk to her," I said.

"It's too late for visiting hours even at the local jail," Lyn said.

I pulled out my wallet to give her my card to pay for my food. Mark grabbed the chips I'd ordered and put them all neatly in a bag, folding the top of the paper bag down carefully.

I fumbled around and found a dollar to put in the tip jar. Mark worked hard and I wanted to be sure he knew I appreciated it. And maybe it was a bit of guilt for all the times I hadn't stood up for him in school.

I waved and exited. Isaac and his family had certainly gotten around the community. They weren't any more popular than Eric. I climbed in my car and headed off for home. It wasn't far but after making the mistake of walking to the police station with Mason, I just wanted to get home, eat, and relax.

14

Thursday is my short day. I get up and get the café opened. I work with my Thursday part-time employee, Joyce. At noon, Greg gets there and I leave. Joyce works with Greg until closing. It's a long day for her, but she was the one who requested the schedule.

I usually come back around closing. While Joyce can and does settle the cats in for the evening, I'm a bit of a micro-manager when it comes to the familiars. I know I'll hear it about it from Mason if the cats aren't well cared for.

If I'm late, Mason relaxes in the main room, enjoying having all the perches and toys to himself. They are clearly his territory though he shares them with the other familiars. And from there, he has the perfect place to supervise Joyce or Charlene, who also helps with the familiars.

I hadn't slept well for the second night in a row. At some point, that was all going to catch up with me and I was going to crash hard. The first thing I did after letting the cats out and cleaning kennels was make an extra-large coffee. I needed to perk myself up.

Natalie and I were planning to have lunch together, right

after we went to the jail to talk to Trinity and find out what was going on. If, for some reason, we couldn't talk to Trinity, we were going to check in with Tyson to find out what was happening. I was hopeful he'd come in that morning, but he wasn't among the coffee buyers.

I still had plenty of people in the café, but not the crowds of the day before. Joyce is particularly fast at pulling drinks so I worked the register. It was a nice change from yesterday. Although the choice to leave Greg at the register was all mine, that didn't mean I wasn't glad to not be working the espresso machine again today.

When I got a break, I cleaned up the back and chatted with Joyce. She's a little younger than I am but married with a baby. Her husband works at home on Tuesdays and Thursdays. Tuesday is Joyce's day to run errands without having to worry about the baby and Thursday is her day to work, though she works part-time on Saturday with me, too.

Her mom babysits on Thursday for her, which means her husband doesn't have a full day to try and juggle baby needs with work.

I have to admit I rather envied her set up. Joyce has a feline familiar, a tuxedo cat named Hannibal. He was kind of a wild cat, particularly as familiars go, but he was a devoted boy. She never had to worry about what was going on at home on Tuesdays because Hannibal kept a very close eye on how attentive her husband was with the baby.

"It's like he thinks he's supervising the whole childcare thing. A couple of times I didn't immediately pick up Kaitlyn when she cried and Hannibal was right there, yelling at me," Joyce said once. It made me wonder if I had children if Mason would be as protective. It was hard to imagine. He was such a laid back cat.

"If you need to leave early, I can take care of things," Joyce said a little before I was planning to go.

"Is it that obvious?" I asked.

"You don't usually pace around looking for something to do," Joyce said. Her blonde hair was curled up around her head under a scarf with the café's name on it.

"I'm meeting Natalie for lunch. We're going to go to the jail and see if we can visit Trinity," I said. "If not, we'll go to Tyson's office and see what he says."

"I'd go to the attorney first. That way, if need be, his office can call ahead and save you a trip."

Joyce's father worked for the Witch's Bureau of Investigation cyber-crimes unit, with a specialty in crimes against familiars.

"I'll suggest that to Natalie when she gets here."

Joyce just smiled at me. She knew Natalie, though not that well. But it was hard to avoid the fact that Natalie could be a force all her own, every bit as uncompromising as a tsunami.

Greg came in and got himself set up. Natalie arrived moments later which was probably some kind of record for her. I doubt she'll be that close to on-time at her own funeral. It really told me how upset she was about Trinity.

"Let's go see about visiting," Natalie said, taking my arm.

I told her about Joyce's suggestion. I knew Natalie was going to argue by the look on her face.

"You parked practically in front of Tyson's office," I pointed out. "We might as well go in while we're there. It can't hurt and might speed up the police if they know we're coming to visit Trinity."

"I wanted to surprise them, to make sure they aren't hurting her or something," Natalie protested, but not terribly hard.

I rolled my eyes.

The weather outside was warmer today than yesterday. The slight respite from the high heat was over, unfortunately.

A few clouds to the east looked threatening and I suspected we'd have an afternoon thunderstorm.

I passed Bill Welks from the bank going to get his coffee. I waved and smiled. He smiled back but said nothing. At least everyone had stopped asking me about Trinity.

Tyson's office sat on the far corner of the block beyond ours. The narrow brown brick building that housed his office might have been a townhouse except for the large window in the front with the sign that said Lyons and Lyons, Attorneys at Law. The building was much longer than it was narrow and once you got past the reception area there were two offices down a hallway and a large conference room. Naturally, they had a bathroom and some sort of room where the paralegals did their work as well. The office's law library was upstairs along with a kitchen, another bathroom, and more space for their paralegals to spread out and work. Natalie and I had toured the place with Trinity a few years back.

A bell over the door rang. Mrs. DiAngelo sat working the front desk. While most people go by their first names, Mrs. DiAngelo had been a fixture in Waverton for years. She worked for Trinity's grandfather before he retired and her brothers took over the office. I suspected even the elder Mr. Lyons called her Mrs. DiAngelo and not just because it was polite.

Her hair was gray but her face was smoother than it had any right to be considering her age. I had heard rumors that she used a spell to make herself look younger than she was. I wouldn't be surprised. No plastic surgeon ever did such a good job on a facelift as the youthful look on Mrs. DiAngelo's face.

"I suppose you're here to talk to Tyson about Trinity," she said. A pair of reading glasses hung on a chain around her neck. In all my life, I'd never seen her raise them to her eyes, even when reading. They were like the world's oddest accessory.

"We wanted to make sure we could visit her at the jail," I said.

Mrs. DiAngelo nodded. "I can take care of that. That way Tyson won't be disturbed. The investigator is here giving him her preliminary report."

There was almost a sniff as if she didn't quite approve of the investigation. Or maybe it was Deborah she didn't approve of. Mrs. DiAngelo made her opinions known unless they related to a client at the office. Then she had the world's best poker face and lips like a steel vault.

Much as I wanted to ask more, I knew it would be hopeless. Natalie, however, had other ideas.

"What has the investigator found?" Natalie jumped in. She pushed in front of me. When it was just asking to see Tyson about Trinity, she was happy to let me go first. Now that there was knowledge to be had, she was going to insist.

"You know I can't talk about that," Mrs. DiAngelo said. Her fingers were already on the phone, starting to dial. A headset framed her face so she didn't have to pick up the phone itself. She just needed to dial. I was so used to seeing her with it on that it had never registered that the black thing that reminded me of an old-fashioned headband was actually her headset. It seemed part of her.

"We're her best friends. I'm sure if Trinity knew, she'd be fine," Natalie pressed. I knew Natalie knew better than that, but she was going to push as far as she could get away with.

Mrs. DiAngelo gave her a long look and then went back to calling the station. Natalie's protest didn't even warrant a comment. She spoke on the phone for a minute or so and then pressed a button.

She looked up at us, frowned at Natalie, then turned her

gaze to me. "You're all set." With that, she looked back over at her computer. We were dismissed.

Natalie fumed but I understood why Mrs. DiAngelo had acted the way she did. It was impossible to argue with Natalie when she got in a mood. If I ever needed a receptionist, I wanted someone as good as Mrs. DiAngelo.

15

Natalie drove her car to the police station. Unlike me, who preferred to walk when possible, Natalie drove whenever she went somewhere, even around town. She was absolutely certain it was faster. I still believed there were times when driving wasn't any faster, but after last night, carrying Mason in his carrier, I was starting to think driving might be easier.

Natalie got lucky and pulled into a parking spot on the street across from City Hall. Someone pulled out just as we were getting close to it.

"You have good parking karma," I said.

"I put a spell on the car when I purchased it. Parking luck," Natalie said.

I laughed. Things could be spelled for luck. Natalie had probably focused on parking when she'd spelled her car. My car had spells to keep me from getting into accidents, but I'd never considered one for parking. In a town as small as Waverton, most people don't, but Natalie did have to go out of town now and again. She attended a lot of conferences.

Plus, she checked out other hotels to see what they were offering their guests.

After passing through security, we headed to the desk where Lani Thomas waited. She waved at us. "Mrs. DiAngelo has you all set up. It's downstairs, so take the elevator around the corner."

I hadn't ever been in the elevator around the corner. It sat next to a desk where an officer worked. I vaguely recognized the woman at the desk, but a name didn't immediately come to me. Waverton is small, but not that small.

Natalie pressed the button which only went down and the elevator doors opened for us. Shiny black walls and dark tile greeted us from a space the size of a janitorial closet. A very small closet. The colors on the walls didn't help. Looking up, I noticed even the ceiling was black.

"I'm not normally claustrophobic, but I could learn," I said, looking around.

The elevator, perhaps enjoying my discomfiture, made its way slowly down to the basement which held the jail. Although Trinity had been arrested, she hadn't had a bail hearing yet. I wasn't sure if that was typical or not.

When the doors opened, we stepped out into a small vestibule area with another metal detector and two officers manning it. One sat in a chair reading a book. As the doors began to close behind us, he stood up casually, not caring that he'd been caught reading.

Down there everything was utilitarian, from the cement floors to the plain gray painted walls. Overhead, white panels lined the ceilings, and large fluorescent lights made a buzzing sound. I heard the air conditioning click on but I didn't feel any air. While the basement was cool enough, the air felt stale and still. A light pressure surrounded my head. My arms tingled as if I were too close to another person.

Drawing in a breath and not encountering any problems moving, I realized it was a spell to dampen magical energy.

"Are you here for Trinity?" the standing man asked.

I nodded.

Natalie continued to look around to assess the place.

"Place your personal items in the lockers over there," the officer said. He pointed to the right where gray lockers nearly the same color as the walls sat. I put my purse in one and took the key from the lock. Natalie did the same.

Then we had to walk through the metal detector. We'd already been through one once just to get to the elevator, but apparently, the jail didn't want to take any chances. They had a conveyor belt there too, but if you had to put your personal items away, I wasn't sure what it was for. Of course, maybe the attorneys brought in notepads and stuff.

My soft-soled shoes squeaked on the floors. Natalie's heels tapped gently away. While halls split off to either side, we were led directly ahead and came to a plain metal door, painted gray, of course. I couldn't help but think that a better color scheme would make people happier. I realized no one cared about criminals, but what about the folks that had to work down there?

When the officer opened the door, I saw Trinity sitting at a table. She didn't have handcuffs on, at least. There were four folding chairs, all bolted to the floor. I noted faint sigils glowing. Another dampening spell. While I'd been nervous down there, walking inside, my mind calmed and I felt clearer than I had since I'd learned of Eric's death. Another spell.

No one said a word until we were all seated and the door was closed. I noted a camera in the corner.

"Thanks for coming you guys," Trinity said. She was in a set of beige pants and tunic that reminded me of the world's most boring scrubs. Her hair was pulled back but it didn't have the usual styling. Today, her hair spilled to her shoulders falling every which way despite the band that struggled to keep it away from her face.

"We've been so worried," Natalie stood up to give her a hug.

"No touching," a disembodied voice said over the intercom.

Natalie glared but sat back down. Cowed, perhaps by the fact that someone might come in and escort her out. I also sat down, having gotten up to take my turn in a hug but not having gotten close.

"Thanks," Trinity said. "It's surreal to be here. I was in the café with you two when it happened. At least that's what we think, but there's someone who swears they saw me. While the police investigate magic to see if I was actually killing Eric when you two think you saw me, I have to stay here."

"It could have been someone else magicked to look like you killing Eric," Natalie said.

"They're looking into that, too. The chief said it would be faster if they proved that you weren't taken in by a spell."

"No one's investigated the café," I said. "No one's talked to me other than about what Mason saw."

Trinity shrugged as if she didn't know and had given up on caring. Gone was her easy smile. While there weren't many in the local jail, I could only imagine how depressing it would be to be there.

"I could lose my job just for being accused, you know," Trinity said. "Who would trust me again?"

"When they find the real murderer, everyone will understand that you did nothing wrong," I said. I hoped I was right. "Tyson has Deborah here to investigate your case."

Trinity sniffed, not unlike Mrs. DiAngelo.

"What's that about?" Natalie demanded. "Do we need another investigator?"

Trinity shrugged and sighed. For a moment I thought she wasn't going to answer. Natalie took a breath to say something more but Trinity held up a hand and spoke.

"Tyson used to date Deborah. She's a good investigator but she didn't take their breakup well. I think that she spends more time trying to get back with Tyson than she does investigating cases now. Tim doesn't even use her services any longer," Trinity said.

My heart fluttered, but I tried to control myself. I mean it wouldn't do Trinity any good to know that I was revisiting my youthful crush on her brother just as she was arrested. This was incredibly poor timing to suddenly find myself at loose ends, finally having my café up and running and in a routine that allowed me to think about what it might be like to have a date now and then.

Once this was over, and Trinity was cleared, I was going to start putting myself out there and work on meeting and dating eligible men. These feelings for a guy who hadn't noticed me in all the years we'd known each other wasn't just foolish, it was rather pathetic.

"Has Tim hired someone else?" Natalie asked. She pushed her hand towards Trinity and then pulled it back.

"No. I mean, Deborah's a good investigator. I just think she's got another agenda. I mean in some ways that's good, right? She'll want to get the results that Tyson wants."

"Did you meet a red-haired woman before you left the library?" I asked. "Did you run into anyone while you were there that morning?" I really wanted to know if Trinity recognized either Isaac or Fiona and perhaps that connection might give us a reason they were so intent upon saying she killed Eric.

Trinity was quiet for a few moments, thinking. "Tyson asked me if I had seen anyone that morning, other than Eric. I mean, I always see patrons. Unfortunately, none of them stand out. I think Sarah Meyerson came in that morning but that's pretty normal. Stacy Redding was in too. She's been researching Moline's Syndrome."

"Isn't that where familiars start losing their powers?" Natalie asked, looking at me.

I shook my head no. "It only affects large animals. They start absorbing their own magic and it becomes part of their body. They grow bigger, even if they're adults, but their magic gets weaker. It was named after Josiah Moline who first discovered that it wasn't actually a spell put on the cow he had taken as a familiar. It was actually a disease. It doesn't seem to affect any of the smaller familiars."

"Oh, that's right. Stacy has that lamb," Natalie said, suddenly making the connection.

"It's a sheep, not a lamb," Trinity corrected. "It's like eight years old or something now."

Natalie shrugged. "Anything else unusual about your day?"

"Just the missing book," Trinity said.

"What was it about?" I asked. It wasn't impossible that Eric had found the person who actually did take the book and they killed him. Perhaps knowing the subject more specifically would help.

"It a really old book on breeding magic into ordinary household pets," Trinity said. "Most of the recipes used magic we try to avoid now."

Meaning the spells used negative magic. That wouldn't bode well for the household pet that became a familiar. While we bred familiars to keep the magic strong, sometimes people created a bond with an otherwise ordinary creature. There were things the witch could do to take those creatures as a familiar, to help them use magic. It wasn't done very often any longer, but before the breeding lines had been established, people bonded with animals when they could.

The best feline familiars, we'd found, were bred with ordinary cats. Most of the kittens would be magical in nature, though now and then we'd get an ordinary cat. Someone usually adopted the ordinary kitten at some point. Dogs, we'd found, did best if they were bred familiar to familiar.

Beyond dogs and cats, I wasn't really aware of the best breeding aspects of other types of familiars.

"We need to find someone who's overly attached to an ordinary pet," Natalie said. "That might be a clue."

"We can't search the entire world," I said. "It doesn't need to be someone who lives here."

"But they probably stayed in the hotel," Natalie argued.

"Not if they were within driving distance," I pointed out. "Let's face it. If you were going to steal a rare, magical book would you want any record that you had visited the town where it was?"

Natalie's shoulders slumped. "I don't know how we're going to find anything out."

"I want to know why that boy Isaac insists that he saw Trinity. It's not like he knows her. He shouldn't be that certain," I said.

Trinity perked up at that.

"You know something?" Natalie pressed.

"I'm not sure," Trinity said. "I feel like there may have been emails to the library by someone named Isaac or maybe about him. I can't quite remember though, which is weird because it seems all I'm doing is living the last few days over and over again."

Natalie and I exchanged a look. We'd have to tell Tyson and make sure Deborah knew that. It could be the connection we needed.

The rest of our visit was taken up with trying to talk Trinity out of her funk. I'm not sure how well we succeeded.

Natalie, of course, promised her we'd get her out of this mess as if it was just a matter of sorting out a small misunderstanding.

I gave Trinity a small smile and blew her a kiss as I left. I knew I couldn't offer her magical comfort through it, though I wanted to try, but at least she'd know I cared. By the time we left, even I was depressed. Rather, more depressed.

At least I could go out and talk to people and do something. Poor Trinity was stuck behind bars in that dull gray jail.

16

Natalie and I ended up having lunch at the bar and grill. It's a funky log cabin building with a huge bar and rustic wood siding just on the other side of the Courthouse. It sits on the road that takes you north and west to Louisville, not that anyone went that far. The road was far too narrow and curvy and the speed limit was low enough that you could drive out to the interstate and go all the way to Lexington and cut over on I-64 faster.

The Waverton Bar and Grill had a large parking lot, most of which was paved. The log cabin building was long and low and easy to recognize so it worked well as a landmark for giving directions. Those mostly included, "If you get to the Bar and Grill, you've gone too far."

The dark logs used to fascinate me as a child. Inside, the logs were smooth halves in a brighter pine color. The floors matched the lighter pine, though those were scuffed and marred from decades of shoes. Magic can only protect so much and repair so much. Besides, the worn look was part of the place's charm.

Even the booths and tables appeared to be made of logs,

though I knew that look was mostly fake. While a few booths might have been made of logs, original to the building, most had been created to look that way as part of the décor. A large stone fireplace sat in between the tables and the bar, powered by gas so that no one had to constantly feed wood to keep it going.

On summer days like this one, the fire didn't burn. No sense in making the air conditioning work any harder than it had to. Still, it made the place feel cozy and smaller than it actually was.

I breathed in the scent of cooked meats, and fries. Kylie Moore, who would be a senior at the high school in the fall, showed us to a table and said a server would be right with us. She'd applied at Natalie's but hadn't gotten the job, though she appeared to show us no ill will. I made a mental note about that if she ever applied to the café. Very professional.

While the place wasn't terribly crowded, plenty of other people were already seated. A party of six businessmen had followed us inside. I didn't recognize them, nor did I sense any magic, so I assumed they were ordinaries who had heard about the place and came for a perfect steak. The bar and grill was known for its good quality meats.

Conversations swirled around us, the low rumble a counterpoint to the soft pop music playing in the background, a mash-up of 80s and 90s hits.

"I don't know why we came here," Natalie said. "I'm not sure I can eat."

"Your idea," I said. "I was good with the diner." I had doubted I could eat much even as I'd gotten back in the car. Certainly, a steak would be wasted on me, but they did do an interesting variety of appetizers. Their burgers were huge so I ruled those out.

"I know. But nothing sounded good from there, either.

What do you suppose Trinity is getting to eat?" Natalie asked.

I shook my head. I had no idea what kind of food they served at the jail. She'd have said if she were hungry, though. At least I thought she would. Trinity knew we wanted to help her.

"I still want to know why that kid is so focused on her. Did someone spell him to be so certain?" I asked.

"And did they pick him because they knew his mother and whoever she was with would push for her child to be heard?" Natalie said. "I mean eventually the evidence will come out that Trinity was with us and it was her and not some illusion. No one can do that good of an illusion."

The last was said with a bit of hesitation. If someone were impersonating Trinity they could get away with it, but Natalie and I were the worst people to try that with. We knew Trinity too well and would have noticed something out of character. Even then, the question was why try it. The obvious reason would be that Trinity had planned to murder Eric. If so, then she'd have made sure she wasn't seen killing him.

"So, does that mean someone just needs to delay the case?" I asked. "Even if they didn't live in town, if they lived in the US, they'd be caught. And no matter where in the world they live, the Witch's Bureau of Investigation would catch them if they used magic committing the crime." And here Natalie and I were talking about using magic to disguise themselves as Trinity, so it was a foregone conclusion that they'd be caught, eventually.

"Technically," Natalie said, "if they were seen as Trinity in just a wig and maybe clothing she might wear, someone who didn't know her could mistake them for her."

The server came and Natalie ordered their wings and a cup of their French Onion soup. The soup sounded good so I got their mini quesadilla and added the soup as well. Natalie added a glass of red wine. I just got a soda. I wanted to be clear if we were discussing Trinity's case.

"And then the WBI wouldn't be able to go after them in another country," I said. "Of course, if the killer was the same person who stole the missing book, the council could come after them for that."

"So let's assume that the missing book and the murder are separate…"

I shook my head. "I think that's a huge coincidence."

"What if they only took the book to give Eric a reason to be angry at Trinity?" Natalie suggested. "Then, the police would be certain to show witnesses images of Trinity. I mean, they probably would anyway because she worked there."

"And the murderer didn't know Trinity's schedule so they didn't plan on her having an air-tight alibi which could then be verified with magic."

"Most people in town know we have that morning break that stretches into lunch," Natalie said. "Particularly business people, so it's not likely one of them, no matter if they had a motive to murder Eric."

"That lets Sarah off the hook," I added.

Natalie nodded. I wished I had brought the little notebook I'd started the other night. I had lots to add to it to try and keep my thoughts straight.

"It also lends credence to the idea that it's someone from out of town," Natalie said. "I have a nearly full hotel so there are plenty of suspects."

"We know that Fiona and Isaac and the older woman they were with were in the library," I said. "They aren't completely off the hook, either."

Natalie nodded. "Do we know the whereabouts of anyone else for certain?"

"Mrs. Ainsley came in shortly after I left you guys to make sure the cafe had plenty of bottled water out. She was late for her appointment due to traffic."

"They could have been in town, then, maybe at the library," Natalie said.

"Except Mrs. Ainsley has a walker. I know that Mason felt she had some negativity, like maybe she used questionable spells, but I can't imagine she'd be murdering people."

"Nice old lady," Natalie said smirking a bit. "What better disguise? I mean what if it wasn't the real Mrs. Ainsley and that's what Mason was sensing?"

"He'd know if it were a spell. He's good that way," I said. All familiars could usually tell when a spell was in use. Mason hadn't actually felt the negativity. Jelliane had, which made it just a tiny bit more suspect. But, had Mrs. Ainsley been wearing a magical disguise, Mason would have noticed it and let me know. He was very protective of the familiars in our care.

Natalie bit her lip. "I'll have to go through the entire hotel roster from that day. I mean the police asked for it so they had a better idea of who was in town. I'm sure that Deborah had means to hack into the system and get it, too, but just in case, I ought to go over it and see what I can come up with."

I nodded. It was a good idea. "There are people who just come for the day which you don't have access to. Like the witch that was in my café. She was clearly untrained and with a bunch of ordinaries, so I expect she doesn't have a clue she's a witch. I reported her to the council, but what if she did more than just make trouble in the café?"

Flori's attitude was bad enough that I could completely see her trying to slip all her friends into the library. Ordinaries didn't normally notice the specialty library. Flori would have been immune to the magic, though. If she wanted to check it out, she'd have wanted to bring her friends, or at least her boyfriend. She had a temper, and untrained as she was, she could have murdered Eric accidentally. It didn't explain Isaac seeing Trinity, though.

Our food came and everything smelled wonderful. Though my stomach still felt tied in knots, it started to wake up to the idea of food.

Natalie pushed her spoon through the thick layer of cheese on the top of the onion soup to get a bit of broth. "I'm just not sure how we can find all of the people who were in town that day. Even people who live here sometimes leave town."

"Do you know what type of security the library has?" I asked.

"They have the cameras on the door," Natalie said after sipping at her soup. She frowned, probably because it was still steaming, and set the spoon aside to pick at her wings.

"Do they have them on the employee doors? Or do we know how Trinity left? A camera should show her leaving. Unless there's a rule about her leaving through the back, it would make sense to leave through the main doors. The café isn't far," I said.

"Tyson should have requested that already," Natalie said. "We really need to talk to him. Let him know we're there to help. I don't care if he has hired that Deborah woman because she's supposed to be the best. We're Trinity's friends and we deserve to know what's going on."

I didn't argue with Natalie about the legalities. I had no doubt she'd just snap at me about backing down too easily.

I bit into my quesadilla. The flavors of the cheese, onions, and tomatoes burst in my mouth. My stomach completely woke up and threatened to rebel if I didn't immediately feed it more. I ate in silence for a bit, companionable with Natalie.

We talked of other things, though our conversations often

circled around to Trinity. There had to be something we could do to help.

"Have you talked to LaRue?" I asked. LaRue was Natalie's familiar cat. She was a petite gray and white tabby cat. She could often be found snoozing on one of the chairs in the hotel lobby, usually in the sun, but sometimes she roamed the hotel corridors.

"I always talk to LaRue," Natalie said. "I haven't asked her specifically about Eric's death because she wasn't there. I did mention it, but she didn't see a spirit like Mason."

"Has she said anything about any of the guests?" I pressed. The quesadilla was gone and I was scraping the last of the cheese from the edges of the bowl my soup was in. LaRue was very opinionated about the guests.

"She hates the kid Isaac," Natalie said, "but that's just in agreement with everyone else. Did you know he chased her around the lobby when they were getting checked in and even tried to get in behind the counter because she jumped over the desk to get away from him? I didn't hear about it until later. Fortunately, Bobbie was working and he's not the sort you argue with."

Tall and heavyset with a shaved head, Bobbie looked more like a bouncer for a strip club than a hotel manager. He was sweet but he knew how to use his looks to his advantage. If he said you weren't going to get in behind the counter, you wouldn't be getting in behind there.

"Tracks with the rest of the town," I said.

"There are about six guests she's not fond of right now," Natalie said. "Your Mrs. Ainsley is on that list, but Isaac tops it. She's avoiding two women from New York who are touring through Kentucky looking for their ancestors. I guess one is certain she's from Waverton. Thinks she knows more than she does about familiars and was a bit too friendly with LaRue to start."

I mentally added them to my list of suspects. Familiars are generally good judges of character. If LaRue didn't like them, no matter the reason, they could have been up to something more than their ancestor search.

"And then there's a solitary man visiting. I'm not even sure why. He's not talkative. I think I asked him something about his visit when I checked him in and he just glared at me like I was being rude. I have no idea where he's from other than he speaks English with a Chicago accent."

Natalie and I paid our bill and headed out. Not a moment too soon. Red-haired Fiona entered along with her son Isaac. The older woman was with them. Isaac's hair was blonder and less red than Fiona's, his face still rounded and chubby from a bit of baby fat. His blue eyes darted around the room, taking everything in, a glint of trouble barely hidden in them. The tension in his muscles suggested a need to move quickly and probably in a direction to make trouble.

Isaac focused on me and Natalie and he began to scream so loudly that I jumped and practically backed into Natalie.

17

I took a step back as if to shield myself from the shrill scream Isaac was making. He still stared at me as if he couldn't pull his eyes from my face. Fiona glared at me, trying to pull Isaac behind her. I was trying to get away from the kid, not harm him, and yet, somehow, she seemed to think otherwise.

Poor Kylie stood at the hostess position, next to a tidy black podium where people checked in for seats. An older couple sat on a bench nearby. The place was about half-full, the lunch hour nearly passed.

Not many people were in the bar area, just a young guy sitting at the long counter talking to the bartender, or he had been until Isaac started screaming. As Natalie and I moved to the door, I'd been listening to the pleasant drone of conversation, but that had stopped the minute Isaac started screaming.

Actually, I couldn't be certain they'd stopped. Isaac's voice was so loud that fifty drummers could have set up shop in the place challenging each other to a drum-off and I wouldn't have heard them. If he wanted, Isaac had a future in Hollywood screaming for horror movies.

I felt a hint of magic floating around, trying to latch onto something. I put up a shield against it. Fortunately, there are certain magical protections that feel almost automatic to me. If it hadn't been nearly automatic, I wouldn't have been able to do a thing. The screeching seemed to stop all activity in my brain.

I noted Natalie's hands moving slightly around her like she was brushing off a spider web. She was probably doing her own warding and automatically motioning something out of her way. No doubt she was as rattled as I was.

Finally, Natalie found her voice. "Shut UP!" I felt the force of the spell drift over me. It headed right to Isaac.

"How dare you use magic on my child!" Fiona yelled. Her voice was almost as loud as Isaac's though she was speaking in words not just screams. "He's clearly terrified."

"Of what?" Natalie demanded. "He wasn't afraid of me earlier at the hotel. There's no reason to be terrified now."

Behind me there was silence. I could feel dozens of eyes all watching what was going on. Kylie's face had turned pink with embarrassment. She rubbed her fingers on the edge of the podium where she'd been standing, trying to smile, but failing. I knew she was trying to think of something to say.

She was saved by Steve Berman who came out of the back. In gray trousers and a white button-down shirt and tie, he looked every inch the manager. His blonde hair was slightly messed as if he'd just run his hands through it. Maybe he had if he'd been concentrating on something when Isaac started screaming. He did not look pleased.

Kylie looked over at him and her cheeks turned pinker. I hoped that he wouldn't be angry with her for not being able to handle this. I'm not sure how I'd handle it if it were in my café.

"He's clearly afraid of the woman you're with. She must have done something. And if you're throwing around spells, taking away a person's voice, I'm sure she's been dabbling in negative magic. Isaac is very sensitive."

My eyes widened. I bit back a plethora of words that I wanted to shout at Fiona.

"I've done nothing wrong," I finally spit at her. "Your son started screaming at me for no reason."

I wanted to add just like he'd accused Trinity of murder. Isaac was standing back by his mom, a satisfied look on his face. I thought I saw something move behind his eyes, something not childlike. A shadow. It made me shiver. Could something have possessed him and he'd murdered Eric?

I shivered a bit.

"I can't have you disrupting my patrons," Steve said, arriving at the podium.

"If you weren't hosting negative magic practitioners, he wouldn't have reacted," Fiona said glaring at me. "But this town seems full of them!"

Given that I thought her child might be the one infected with negative magic, it was a rather rich accusation.

"You are accusing two long-time residents and upstanding citizens of practicing negative magic on nothing more than your child's reaction," Steve said quietly, his voice pitched almost in a whisper. He did not look happy. "I'll have to ask you to leave lest he take a dislike to another one of my regular patrons."

Steve crossed his arms and looked at Fiona, waiting. He wasn't backing down.

Fiona argued a bit. Steve refused to give in. Kylie slipped away from the podium with a couple of menus and seated the couple who had been waiting. The busboy who had been cleaning peeked out of the kitchen, watching. The bartender leaned over and looked at us. A few of the patrons had gone back to eating, but others continued to watch. Even the ones trying to eat kept glancing back over here, wondering what was going on.

I didn't recognize everyone. I hoped there weren't too many ordinary people in the bar and grill. Fiona practically screaming about negative magic wasn't exactly discrete and we weren't supposed to talk about being witches in public.

It was definitely a lapse in judgment, but perhaps not so much that the council would fine her even if it was brought to their attention. Still, she was walking a line.

"I can't believe you're not going to seat us. We're upstanding visitors to your community. I'm well known in my own area and if I say 'don't visit Waverton,' people will listen," Fiona argued. "Particularly if I warn them about the rampant negative magic."

"We have visitors from all over the world, ma'am," Steve replied. "I'm sure that if your community can do without the unique expertise in our little town, that there are many others who won't feel the same way. Given that you have no proof of any sort of wrongdoing, we'll take our chances. If you continue your allegations, I shall have to call in the council to witness."

Fiona glared at him. "How dare you say I have no proof! Isaac is all the proof I need." She took her son's hand and turned. The old woman followed them. She'd said nothing during the incident, but had stood solidly beside Fiona, a mere witness who didn't wish to get involved.

"I'm sorry," Steve apologized to Natalie and me. He pulled out some coupons. "I hope you'll come back again and continue to refer to the bar and grill." The last was spoken directly to Natalie. I had no doubt that the next time Natalie came in, Steve would know and he'd make sure to comp her meal. I was somewhat surprised that he hadn't comped this one, but we'd already paid. He'd been slow enough in arriving that perhaps he'd even looked up what we ordered and knew we'd not eaten much.

"Thanks," we both said, pausing to let Fiona and Isaac time to leave before we got out of the bar and grill.

Even after leaving the place, we huddled at the door, looking out at the parking lot. We watched Fiona and her family get in the car. They weren't parked far from ours. Neither Natalie nor I had any desire to run into them again.

"Something is definitely up with them," Natalie whispered.

"I thought I saw a shadow go past Isaac's eyes. I had the thought that maybe he's possessed."

"And maybe whatever possessed him murdered Eric?" Natalie asked.

I nodded.

"Sounds about right to me," Natalie said. "We really need to meet with Tyson and let him know. He can make sure the police check on that kid and check him for possession." In another town that would sound like she thought Isaac was using drugs. In Waverton, like other witchy towns, it literally meant possession, like by a negative entity of some sort.

We drove in silence on the way back. Natalie got a phone call from the hotel. Apparently, there'd been an issue with the laundry and she was needed.

"I guess you'll have to see Tyson on your own," Natalie said.

"I'll see what I can do," I said. "It's not like anything will happen right away. I mean, this is almost a council issue now and you know the police aren't going to appreciate that."

Natalie sighed. "So they'll drag their feet." She humphed again, clearly displeased. A few moments later she let me out in front of the café.

I watched her drive away, wondering about Fiona and Isaac and the mysterious older woman who was always with them. I fiddled with my phone, hoping to get into see Tyson. Mrs. DiAngelo said she'd leave him a message. I tapped my foot, not surprised, but definitely disappointed.

When Greg came in at eight the next morning, I was already busy with customers. It wasn't anything I couldn't handle, but it seemed that most people in the downtown area decided this was the place to get their coffee. I'd already sold out of the scones I get from Shirley's around the corner. We had some muffins left and their banana bread, but the latter was always a second choice and plenty of people were disappointed.

"What's up with this?" Greg asked.

I shrugged. I hadn't had time to ask or even figure out how to ask.

I moved to pulling drinks and letting Greg get started on the register. There's a bit less work on the register and I liked to give him a bit of time to wake up. As people weren't here to ask me about Trinity—thank the heavens—I was good trading off in a half an hour or so. My wrists and arms would thank me later.

"So what's going on?" I heard Greg ask over the low music and the roar of the espresso machine.

"Shirley's is closed," Mia Jorgensen said. She was an

older woman who worked up at the bank three days a week. I waved at her as I pulled a mocha latte for the young man who had just ordered. We were keeping up, but just barely.

"Really?" Greg said. "Is she sick?" He glanced at me.

I shrugged.

"She had a break-in late last night," Mia said. Her silver hair was clipped short around her ears but it still moved as she did.

"That's horrible," I added. I couldn't believe that everyone in here wanted the bakery.

"And the coffee shop a few blocks over by the courthouse just didn't open," Mia added. "I'm worried about Paulette."

I nodded. Paulette had been invaluable in working with me on what I needed for the cat café. I'd been surprised she was so willing to be open about what would make a good café, but as she said, I was opening a familiar café which would draw a completely different crowd than she did.

There were definitely people who went to her shop to do some work, too, and the familiar café wasn't as friendly towards people who just wanted to work. With the visitors coming and going to see the cats, the place was a bit noisier in fits and bursts so the chat wasn't as easy to tune out.

"Has anyone called her?" I asked from where I worked the machine. Mia brought her plain coffee over. Shirley served plain coffees in three flavors each day. She had two regulars and one she rotated as the Coffee of the Day.

"Not that I'm aware," Mia said. "I'm running late to the bank, otherwise I'd call her myself."

"I'll see you around noon," I said.

Friday was my day to take the bank receipts over. Normally, either Greg or I took them over at the end of the day and put them in the drop. On Fridays, I went by at lunch so that I could buy some change. I'd gotten pretty good at it so that I wasn't often going over sooner to get more change to keep in the safe.

"It's Friday, isn't it?" Mia said shaking her head. "It's so easy to get confused sometimes. Yes, I'll see you later."

I didn't have time to watch as she left. Three other people came in. They had an appointment that morning to meet the familiars. They weren't using magic, so I didn't get any sensation about who they were. I let my magical sense search out and felt the core inside them. They were all witches. I liked the feel of the young man in the blue shirt and shorts. I hoped he was one of the people looking for a feline familiar.

Greg took their drink orders and got them set for the room, going over the rules and mentioning that we needed to go into the feline room first. I noted that this was a new part of the speech, probably something he'd incorporated after the incident with Flori and her friends. Hopefully, the kids wouldn't be returning.

The young man in blue ordered a plain tea, the other man, older and perhaps his father or an uncle, ordered a chai, and the older woman with them ordered a plain coffee. I made the chai while Greg got the hot water for tea and let the young man pick out a teabag. Then he got the coffee. By that time, I had the chai ready.

Greg stayed at the cash register while I got them settled in the cat room.

I paused to give Mason a chin rub. In return, I got a large purr from him. Jelliane was already out and sniffing at the new people. Kitika wasn't jumping on laps, but she was out, which was always a good thing. Hopefully, she'd take a liking to the young man. I liked the way his energy felt and she needed a kind witch to bond with—and a young one, too.

Greg was working the register amidst another flurry of activity. Six people came in, all separate, but following through the doors.

"I can't believe that you don't have another coffee place," the woman said. I sensed no magic around her and got the impression she was from out of town. "I just stopped on my way north. Thought I'd take the scenic route because there's a major accident on 75 up near Lexington. But no coffee except for a cat café?" She sneezed. "I'm allergic."

Fortunately, she only wanted a regular coffee and we got that for her quickly to get her out of the café. I didn't need someone in there grumbling about the amenities in town, or lack thereof.

It was nearly lunch before people stopped coming through the door in waves. I suspected they all went to other places first and then someone had the idea that Jade's Café has coffee and they'd all headed here, following each other like sheep.

Greg and I started cleaning up the back area where we served coffee. We'd run out of muffins and banana bread. I'd have nothing for later on. I couldn't even call Shirley if she'd had a break-in. She was probably working with the police and with repair people to get things fixed.

"I wonder what's going on at Shirley's," I murmured.

"I can run over there," Greg said. "Talk to her. She's a good friend of my mom's."

Shirley was friendly and knew just about everyone. I'd consider her a friend but perhaps not a "good friend." Besides, it was Greg's turn to get some time off.

"Go ahead. If she's got anything she can sell us, grab it," I said. I didn't expect that to be the case, but I could be wrong. Shirley liked to bake when she was upset and I couldn't imagine something more upsetting than having your business broken into. And if people couldn't go into her shop, then she needed to sell her baked goods somewhere.

Shortly after Greg left, another customer came in. The people visiting the familiars finished their time and another group arrived. As the group left, the young man in blue came over. "I really enjoyed my time here. The long-haired black cat, I think, said her name was Kitika?" he paused waiting for my acknowledgment.

I nodded, smiling. I didn't quite clap my hands together but it took a great deal of effort. Knowing her name meant that she'd been willing to let him into her telepathic world. A very good sign that they were both willing and able to bond. While Kitika had liked Mrs. Ainsley, if she'd offered her name, I hadn't heard about it.

"Can I put in an application on her?"

I wanted to jump up and down. While I hated that Kitika was going to be out of town and I would have to work harder to check up on her, I was glad that she'd made a choice. I liked her choice, too.

I got the paperwork set up and then went to help a couple of other people who came in for coffee. John Morse, who worked at City Hall, came in. My heart sank seeing him, not that I didn't like him. John's a friendly young man. It just meant that the coffee shop wasn't open yet. After ordering, John noted the young man filling out information on Kitika and started talking to the group. Never let it be said that our city workers aren't friendly.

While I made John's coffee, a latte with a shot of hazelnut flavor, I heard that the family was from Georgetown, just north of Lexington. Ian, the young man, was their son. They'd been looking for a feline familiar for him for some months. They'd gone to breeders but none of the cats had really bonded with Ian. They'd come here as sort of a last-ditch effort before branching out into other familiars.

"We're just cat people," the woman said, looking down at Ian. "His first cat was a beautiful Siamese but she died about a year ago. I know that's probably part of the problem. The first bond is always the most intense. I was worried about an older cat who had had another witch, but Kitika seemed to like all of us. And if I were looking, I'd have fallen in love with that little calico she has in there, too and then we'd both be filling out forms."

Good. They were a feline familiar household and knew about cats. Kitika was one very lucky cat.

"Hey John," I called out handing him his latte.

"Thanks," he said.

"The coffee shop still closed?" I asked.

John winced and glanced over. He leaned forward. "They found Paulette in the back. She'd been hit over the head. Took her to the hospital a bit ago. The worker who was called in can't do a thing because it's clearly a crime scene."

"Oh dear," I said. "I hope she's going to be okay."

John nodded. His face was grim and I worried we'd have another death on our hands.

Greg hurried back in just as John left.

"Well?" I asked. I was keeping my voice soft. Ian was still working on his application. The music was on low, old pop music on instrumentals, but the café seemed too quiet after the morning rush with all the talking and gossip that had gone on. It was too bad I couldn't have just sat there and listened to what everyone was saying. Someone might have known something about Eric's death.

"Shirley couldn't get in until about an hour ago, but she's baking now. She'll bring over some scones and muffins for later, just a small batch. She knows we don't have a lot of business this late," Greg said putting his apron back on as he slipped back behind the counter.

"Did she say what happened?" I asked. We'd been lucky to not get hit. It would have been incredibly upsetting if the familiars had been put in any danger. Mason would have let me know and I'd have gone running down, but still... the idea.

"Someone broke in and tried to get into her safe, but they

weren't able to. They took all her day-old stuff and a picture of Man O'War that she had in the little dining area."

"Really? That's all?"

"She thinks that they were looking for money but they got hungry so took the day-old stuff when they couldn't get into the safe. Maybe they were horse lovers?" Greg shrugged. It was an odd robbery.

"No one was hurt?"

Greg shook his head and leaned closer. Ian and his family were whispering together about something on the application. They were all smiling a bit, so maybe it was a good memory.

"I heard Paulette was found over at the coffee shop," Greg hissed.

"I heard that too, from John," I told him. "Did Shirley know what happened there?"

"Another break-in, looks similar to what happened at her place, but they must have gotten to the coffee shop later and Paulette came in and surprised them. She was hit over the head. They had less day-old stuff but that was taken as well," Greg said. "Someone was really hungry."

"Or had a lot of people to feed," I said. Both Paulette and Shirley knew their businesses so there wasn't a ton of day-old items floating around. Still, it would be enough to feed maybe half a dozen people for breakfast quite well.

"No money?" I double-checked.

"Once again, fooled by the safe," Greg said. "I did hear that they found some residual magic on the dial so someone was hoping they could magically break-in."

"That's stupid." Everyone knew that any magical business put spells on their safes to keep an unscrupulous witch from breaking in and taking their earnings. It was like magic 101 or something.

"I'm thinking drugs," Greg said.

Ian brought up the application. I thanked him and took it. I was looking forward to calling the veterinary references on the family and then the personal references. There was a three-day waiting period to pick up the familiar. It gave everyone a chance to change their minds.

"Are you staying in town or driving home?" I asked them.

"Driving back home. We had a room in the hotel last night but they're booked solid so we can't extend our stay. I can't believe how many people visit here. I didn't even think to reserve more nights," Ian's mother said. Ian looked uncomfortable as only a twenty-something young man can look when his mother started chatting.

"Summers get busy. Normally it's cooler here than down in Lexington or Louisville and it's pretty, so anyone who knows about Waverton schedules their visits around now," I said. "The people are still here even though the weather isn't exactly cooperating."

"I think it is a bit cooler than it is in Lexington. Our house overlooks a little lake and there are plenty of trees so we can avoid the worst of it," she said, smiling. "I hope everything works out. I'd have loved to come back and visited some more with Kitika before then."

"I have slots for potential adopters to revisit after hours. If you end up finding a place closer and decide to stay longer, just give us a call and we'll be sure to fit you in." I sent out a bit of my magical sense and touched the woman. She had the same nice velvety-soft energy her son had. Kitika was going to a very nice home.

The three of them left and I was about to go in and see Mason when Mrs. Ainsley slowly made her way inside with her friends.

"Mrs. Ainsley!" I said. "You should have let us know you'd be back."

"I figured that you'd know how much I liked Kitika. I had

to go check on my options but I'm here to put in an application."

"Well…" I hesitated not quite sure how to put it. I'd not had that experience before. Even in the shelter things like this tended to work out. "I just had another application put in for her. I can take your information and if something doesn't check out I can start on yours." I smiled, hoping that was enough.

Mrs. Ainsley didn't appear to react. She just stood there, hands on her wheeled walker, looking straight ahead. Her face might have been carved of stone. Finally, she drew a breath and spoke. "When did they visit her?"

"Just this morning, but it was an instant connection," I said.

"Then I saw her first and my application should be the one you take," Mrs. Ainsley said.

"Quite honestly, I think this family is a good fit for Kitika. It's a young man. Her prior witch died suddenly and she's had a difficult time of it. I'd rather have her go to a family who will love her. That way if something should happen to her witch, not only is she cared for, but she's surrounded by people she already knows."

"You're a fool," she snapped, glaring at me. She drew herself up straighter. Suddenly she seemed more powerful than the bent old woman.

"I'm in charge of the familiar café and if that's your reaction, I don't believe I'm comfortable adopting out any of my cats to you," I said.

Mrs. Ainsley pointed a finger at me. I felt the magic start around me. I started to put up a shield but her magic was stronger than expected and faster. Fortunately, Greg was watching all this and he added a shield around the whole counter which deflected almost all the magic. I felt like someone had pushed me back a few feet, but I managed not to fall.

"That's it," I said. "You need to leave now." I sent an urgent magical message to Lani at the police station. Hopefully, someone would respond quickly enough. Paulette should have been able to do that unless she was knocked out before she realized anyone was there.

Mrs. Ainsley stood there staring at me. "You'll regret this," she hissed at me. The other women with her appeared not to notice anything amiss. Mrs. Ainsley sank back into herself, just an old woman with a walker slowly pushing her way out of the café.

Tom Alsez arrived, double parking in front of the café, and hurried in.

I pointed at Mrs. Ainsley.

"Her?" Tom mouthed. I nodded.

Mrs. Ainsley kept slowly walking away as if she hadn't a clue that I might have summoned the law. Tom looked back at her, eyebrows raised.

"What happened?" he asked.

I sighed, trying to figure out what to say. Greg had no such problem.

"She wanted to fill out an application for a cat that had just been adopted, or was about to be, and then she got mad. She told Jade she'd regret this and pointed her finger. I had a spell ready when she started getting mad. I don't know... maybe it was a feeling? Anyway, when she pointed at Jade, I let fly and got a spell up. Even so, I felt the force of it. She was mad. And she's dangerous. I think she might even have cursed the place, just a bit," Greg said.

While Greg isn't quiet, that was the most I'd ever heard him talk at one time. He was practically breathless.

"And then, she just stooped back over," Greg said, "like nothing happened."

Tom frowned. "We'll have an officer watching this

evening. With the other break-ins and Eric's death, I don't want to leave anything to chance."

"Thanks," I said.

"And I'd re-do your magical protect spells around the building, too. Call the landlord and have him do his own," Tom advised.

Good advice on both counts. I looked at Greg. "Let's do some spells while it's quiet. We can close down for a bit while we work."

Greg turned the open sign to closed and I pulled the blinds. It didn't give us perfect privacy but an ordinary person walking by wouldn't necessarily notice what was going on. And it seemed important not to put this off. Mrs. Ainsley's transformation had really shaken me.

2 0

I had plenty of salt in the back. I always had cloves for special coffee treats and I thought I had some coriander. All herbs that I could use in a protection spell. After digging those out, I found the candles that I kept on hand. Then I grabbed Mason to help me focus even more.

Greg had moved tables to the center of the room. The reason no one would expect we were doing magic was because what we were doing didn't look like magic. My magic wasn't ceremonial, but the magic of thought and will. For small magics, such as finding out whether someone was a witch or an ordinary, I didn't need any real focus. It required only the smallest push of magic.

For something like a protection spell on a building, well, that took more concentration. I spread salt along the edges of the room infusing it with my desire to keep the building and all those inside safe. My focus was on the familiars because I knew that keeping myself safe was only a secondary concern.

Greg followed behind using the cloves. When that was done, I lit the three candles I had placed on one of the tables crowded together in the middle of the room. Mason jumped on the table and stared at the candle. I pulled a chair up and sat behind him, my hands running through his soft fur.

Greg sat beside me and placed a hand on Mason's side. We said nothing for a few minutes.

Mason meowed a low plaintive meow. The familiars in the feline room echoed it. Greg and I started to chant the words, "Keep all of us safe," over and over again. I felt the energy building like a funnel rising to the sky. It started moving in a circle and got larger and larger until it filled the room.

At that moment, Greg and I stood together and raised our hands, sending the magic outward towards the walls. Mason's fur raised up along his back. His ears flattened. And then he relaxed with a single mew, sounding like a forlorn kitten.

I breathed out in long breaths. So did Greg. After three long breaths, I felt the magic settling into the walls. Mason's fur was back against his body and he began to wash a paw.

Greg looked at me and I nodded. He snuffed the candles with a wave of his hand. Doing so would send any magic the fire had accumulated during the ritual out into the café. I wanted every drop of magic protecting the place that I could get.

I picked up the spices and took them into the back. Greg started moving tables into their usual spots. Next, I let Mason back into the feline room. He took his time sauntering in, though he knew very well we had a visit scheduled and they were waiting patiently outside. I thanked heavens they were witches and would understand.

When things were mostly picked up, Greg turned the closed sign back to open and unlocked the door. Four women entered for their visit. I felt the magic wafting off of them along with curiosity. They wanted to know why we were performing a ritual when the café should be open. Not a one of them asked. The youngest of them, a dark-haired young woman who was probably still in college raised an eyebrow at me.

I just smiled at her and got them settled in the familiar room. They all had herbal teas, which made their orders easy enough. As they settled in with the cats, Greg and I got back to clearing the tables and finishing setting them in order. The salt and cloves along the edges of the room had faded into the woodwork with the spell. Good. The spell had done its job.

"I'd do sigils, too," the dark-haired woman said leaving the familiar room.

"Hmm?" I asked.

"I can feel your protection spell. Something happened earlier or you wouldn't have closed things up to do a spell. If there's immediate danger, I'd add sigils. You can do it tonight. A familiar like your ginger and white cat has enough power to help you," she said.

My eyes opened wide and I looked around. The girl wasn't wrong, but her accuracy about what we were doing was uncanny.

"Sorry," she said. It wasn't really polite to let another witch know you knew what she was doing, but in her case, she was just trying to help. "I'm not very powerful but I do have a talent for knowing the best spells or magic for a situation. I don't even have to try."

I'd heard of such talents. Thankfully I wasn't blessed with such a thing. Often those witches become sort of Cassandra-ish figures who have a general sense of what's wrong and what needs to be done, but people tend not to listen.

I probed just a tiny bit, not so much that I'd be considered rude for doing so, and found that her energy seemed solid and kind. She had no other motives beyond wanting to share what she saw and knew.

"I like cats," she said, clearly feeling my small probe.

"As do I," I said.

"I can feel that, too, though it's not magic. It's part of what makes up this situation, though I'm not sure how. Remember later, sigils," she said.

"Are you looking for a familiar?" I asked. I mentally perused the familiars I had to try and think of who would be a good fit.

The girl shook her head. "We thought the idea of the familiar café was interesting. I wanted to see how it was done and how the familiars liked it. They do, actually. I didn't think cats would."

"They always have the option of a time out in the back if they want," I said. "And I do try and vet the people coming in. It's harder with ordinary people because I have to find an excuse, but with others, I can be honest. And really, with ordinary people, Mason will fill in and purr at them. They might be disappointed that he's not up for adoption, but they usually understand."

"Something is going on in Waverton," the girl said. "I feel some negativity going around. You're not the only one doing protection spells. People have been hurt, too. It's not normally like this. I've visited before when I was looking at colleges."

"We've had someone murdered. In the library," I said.

"I feel like there are many tangled threads. You're trying to find a point to investigate. You are right and wrong in one of the people you're considering. I feel like they are a focal point but that it's really about something else. Like people watching a magician, you know it's him but you don't know how or who's helping him."

My jaw must have dropped.

"I should let you be," the dark-haired girl said. "I've prob-ably said too much. I can see the patterns, but not the actors. I'm sorry."

Her face was red and she hurried to the feline room. I was right and wrong. Someone I suspected was behind this, but it wasn't exactly as I thought. I suspected a lot of people but Fiona and Isaac were at the top of my list. I wondered what the twisted thread was that I wasn't seeing.

The young witch's words stayed with me as I tried to fit pieces together. I kept thinking about what she said while I was pulling drinks, cleaning up the main café area, and restocking the cooler in the front. Faintly, I smelled the fresh cloves that now lined the walls.

I noticed that Jelliane and Ned, a tiny black tuxedo cat, were particularly interested in the most recent visitors. I wasn't sure how serious they were about adoption but I appreciated that they gave all the cats some time. Kitika had gone to the back, probably having tired herself out while charming her new owner.

I shuddered at the thought of Mrs. Ainsley. At least the building was protected. I hoped I wouldn't hear any more from the elderly woman. I had alerted the police. Any number of other witches had probably picked up my distress call. The grapevine was likely going wild about her. I wouldn't be surprised if she was asked to leave most of the places she wanted to visit. Waverton is a small town in that respect.

Charlene arrived. Greg got to leave. I closed on Fridays.

Friday afternoons were usually slow and I probably could have handled it myself, but Charlene needed hours and I needed help just often enough that it made it worthwhile to have another person in the shop. I let Charlene start cleaning litterboxes and filling food dishes even though there was still a group in the room. Charlene could work from the back and not disturb them too much. When the last group of visitors left, I went in and had Mason get the cats to settle in their spaces.

The wards feel strong, Mason said. *You and Greg put a lot of good effort into them. It would be an unusual witch who could cause problems now.*

Unusual was a good way to put it. Either very powerful or very negative, in other words. Fortunately, we didn't see that kind of thing very often.

"At least the last groups seemed nice enough. What did you think of the dark-haired girl? The one that came out to talk to me during her visit," I asked. I figured Mason would have a take and it might give me a clue about how far to trust her.

She's not very powerful, Mason said. *But I sensed a good heart. And much hurt. Is that what she wanted to talk to you about?*

I told him what she had told me.

I believe her. What part of you 'have it wrong and right' do you think she meant? Mason asked.

"I don't know. I mean, her words weren't really helpful, although I guess I am on the right track. I've been focused on Fiona and Isaac, so maybe I am right about them but not the way I think?"

Think about your conversation so I can hear exactly what she said, Mason ordered.

I thought about our conversation, trying not to put words in the girl's mouth. Mason could sort through the memories of what was correct and what I might have added to the conversation or changed to suit my understanding.

You are right about one of the people you think did it, but also wrong, Mason said. *She describes the situation as that of a magician. What aren't you seeing? Where is the trick?*

It probably went back to Fiona and Isaac, but again, I didn't know what I was missing about them. I wondered if perhaps Isaac's bad behavior was a trick to keep people from noticing something else. I thought about the older woman who seemed to blend into the background but whenever I'd seen them, she'd been there. I just didn't notice her. I didn't even know her name. When I thought about her, I realized I had a hard time picturing her. I wondered if she'd done a spell to keep people from paying attention to her.

I left the feline room. Charlene continued the evening cleaning while Mason supervised from his perch. She'd wipe down the perches and make sure all the toys were picked up and then vacuum the floor. We'd run a mop around the room after.

I went to find my cell phone but a couple of late afternoon coffee drinkers came in. I wasn't surprised when one ordered herbal tea and the other ordered a decaf latte. When they had their drinks, they went to the back of the café to sit at a table. I wondered if it was a first date meeting or perhaps a work meeting. I recognized the man, though I didn't know him personally, but not the woman.

I watched their chat, noting the body language for a few moments, and decided it was a job interview. Having satisfied my curiosity about the couple, I called Natalie.

"What's up?" Natalie said when she answered. I heard people talking in the background and the slight echo of words. She was probably at the front desk.

"You're working," I said. "I can call back."

"I'm good," Natalie replied. "The front desk person has it in hand now. They needed some help with a little situation."

"Oh?"

"The grapevine says that you had to call for help and it had to do with Mrs. Ainsley. I may have accidentally booked someone else in her room after tonight. We just had to apologize to her and let her know her visit was cut short," Natalie said. I heard the glee in her voice.

"Was she as nasty to your worker as she was to me?" I asked.

"She acted like a hurt old woman and slightly confused. The other two women were rather angry at us. It was only when nothing came of their interventions that Mrs. Ainsley went all multiple personality change on us and became some horrible entitled creature." The sounds around Natalie had changed and I now heard the soft music that she had playing around the public areas of her hotel.

"Did she threaten the hotel?" I asked.

"Nope," Natalie said. "She just said we were all stupid and she couldn't believe such a mistake had been made. I think she really believes we are just that stupid and made a mistake. For right now, it doesn't seem to have occurred to her that we'd have heard and made note of your call for help to the police. Quite the piece of work there. I did comp her tonight's room for her trouble, which I'm sure will help."

"I hate that you did that," I said. Mrs. Ainsley was no one's friend.

"I'm fine with it. It's worth it if it gets rid of her sooner. Imagine what she could do to a guest. Not all our guests are witches and if she let fly a curse, someone could get really hurt, not to mention she'd break council rules and there'd be a huge investigation." Natalie sighed. An investigation would be a pain because the hotel would be under scrutiny to be sure that they weren't at fault somehow. As if they were forcing a customer to use magic in front of others. It sounded ridiculous to me, but Natalie said it had happened.

"I had a weird encounter," I said. I told Nat about what the dark-haired girl had told me.

"So basically we're on the right track but we're off on the hows and whys," Natalie summarized.

"Or something like that. I kind of think that this revolves around Fiona and Isaac," I said.

"The question is, do they even know how it revolves around them?" Natalie asked. "If the girl is right, we're wrong about something. We just don't know what. I wish people like that witch had better clues when you need to know something."

"I'm sure she's wished that more than once. Can you imagine having that talent? I'd hate it," I said.

"My mother's great aunt had it," Natalie said. "I know Mom worried that one of us kids would be stuck with it. It's not fun. And it's certainly not fun when we have a clue from someone like that, but don't know how to use it."

"Well, we should probably continue to find out what we can about Fiona and Isaac," I said.

"I'm off soon. I'll come by. Stay at the café until then so I can find you," Natalie said.

"Mason is going to want to go upstairs. He gets lonely down in the café. It's only sort of his space, you know."

"Then take Mason home and come back down. There's always more parking in the front when it gets late," Natalie said. "We're going out again."

I hung up the phone wondering what sorts of adventures Natalie had in mind.

22

Mason was safely ensconced upstairs with a large bowl of food and some extra kibble. The café was spotless and Charlene had left for the night leaving me to wait for Natalie while my body screamed for the coffee that was a permanent smell around the café. If the pots weren't already washed and ready for the morning, I'd have given in.

I paced around the room, the chairs already up on the tables for the evening. Charlene had mopped while I counted money. A perk of being the manager. I'd missed lunch because with everything going on, I'd barely had time to get to the bank and purchase my change. I'd had one of our late scones to tide me over. What I really wanted now was to go upstairs and have a huge sandwich or better yet, be on my way someplace to pick up something to gorge on while I watched a movie with Mason.

I noted Natalie's car pulling up in front, and hurried out, pausing only to turn off the main lights and re-lock the door.

"I'm starving," I said.

"We're meeting Tyson at Shim's," Natalie said.

Shim's was the steakhouse that overlooked the valley that Waverton was in. It wasn't actually in incorporated Waverton but it was considered part of the town. It helped that it was run by witches, both of whom had strong studies in the hospitality industry. Len and Franny Dooley were the owners. My parents knew them slightly. Natalie's family knew them better, which wasn't a surprise. Both families were in the hospitality business and the friendship, no doubt, benefited both.

"What?" I asked. I wasn't dressed. I was in cream-colored denim pants and a short-sleeved blue top. I had worked all day in that top. I'd run down to the bank, and while it wasn't as hot as it had been, the humidity had still managed to bring on the sweat while I was out. I was tired and grimy from doing a spell earlier in the day.

"I didn't want to tell you in case he couldn't meet us, what with Deborah in town. However, she's doing some research out of town tonight and he was free. I think that works out," Natalie said.

"Tyson can't tell us anything. It's all client confidentiality," I protested.

"And I got Trinity to sign a waiver," Natalie replied confidently. "I saw how busy you were today so I didn't come by or ask you to join me. I went in at noon and got it. Tyson can tell us everything that Deborah found."

I frowned. I'd not heard of anything like that, but I'd never been arrested before and had little to do with the justice system. Small legalities like a waiver wouldn't be anywhere on my radar.

"I'm totally not dressed to go to Shim's," I said.

Natalie didn't even spare me a glance. "No one expects you to look perfect. Anyone with any magic knows you had to re-up your protection spells this afternoon."

Which pretty much meant the whole town. Still, it didn't mean I wanted to be seen like that.

"Everyone needs a good meal after a big working. It's fine," Natalie assured me. I noticed she was in nice white slacks, sandals, and a blue and white print blouse that looked filmy and sexy the way it fell around her body. I looked like I'd just slept in a dumpster. A clean dumpster, but a dumpster all the same.

Shim's was situated on a hill that overlooked the town. The road Natalie drove was narrow and crossed a stream running through a gorge. The climb upwards caused the engine of her car to work a bit harder than normal but we made it without incident. The turn to the restaurant was on the right and the parking lot was a large section of blacktop behind the building.

Getting out of the car, I smelled the fresh firs that edged the back of the lot and the sap from some of the broadleaf trees. I heard the sounds of cars driving along the narrow highway we would have connected with in another half a mile up the road.

Natalie and I crossed the parking lot to the modern-looking glass and stone building. The black roof was angled just enough to keep snow from piling too high, with the long side on the back angling a bit more shallowly than the part towards the front. A large wooden deck invited people to step up onto it. The deck itself ran around the side of the building where the main doors were.

The view as you turned the corner was spectacular, the sun setting low on the horizon behind us, shining a pinkish light across the valley where I could make out the downtown area of Waverton. Further on, I noted the hotel where Natalie worked and a few farms that I was familiar with. My family home was too close to this edge of town, tucked into a subdivision that was sheltered by too many trees and the angle of the slope to be seen.

Natalie pulled open the black metal and glass door to the entry. My shoes squeaked on the black tile floor. Natalie's neat heels clicked almost in time with the violin music that played softly.

A blonde woman holding menus opened the inner door for us and we stepped inside. The floors here were covered in deep blue carpet with narrow gold stripes along the edges. The ceiling was high with the furnace vents and pipes open to below giving the place an industrial look.

"Natalie Edgars. Party of three. Two of us are here. We're meeting someone," Natalie told the young woman at the podium, a different woman from the one with the menus.

The woman with the menus conferred with her counterpart and then nodded at us. The menus were set aside. "The rest of your party has arrived," the menu girl said, leading us into the restaurant.

The lights were dim and we were led through a maze of round tables and booths that sat upon risers on the far side of the room. The booths on the other side were pushed up next to a gold railing that allowed a view. Two steps down took us to more booths that sat next to the large windows overlooking the valley.

We were led down those stairs, passing two-top round tables on one side and booths on the other. Tyson was seated at the very back, facing our direction, though he was busy looking at the menu and didn't notice us until we reached the table. A foaming glass of beer sat in front of him. When he looked up and saw us, he gave us a strained smile.

Natalie and I slid into the booth across from him. Menus waited for us on the table, the place settings appropriate. The young woman left us before we could order a drink or anything like that. Not that I planned to drink.

I'd barely nodded at Tyson and said hello while Natalie wiggled around getting comfortable when our waitress came by to get drink orders.

Natalie ordered a wine spritzer. I ordered a Dr. Pepper. I'm not much of a drinker and if we were going to learn what Tyson knew about Trinity's case I wanted a clear head. It's not like Natalie had given me time to go upstairs and grab my notebook, though I probably should have packed it when I took Mason upstairs. I'd really expected it would be just the two of us and we'd be going to the diner, or at best the Bar and Grill, not Shim's.

The waitress disappeared. I'm sure Tyson could watch her walk away from his vantage, but where I sat she just disappeared behind me as if she'd never been, her shoes soundless upon the carpet and the backdrop of murmurs of conversation and soft music.

I smelled garlic and basil. Someone nearby had ordered Italian.

"Let's order, first, shall we?" Tyson said. I noticed Natalie had just opened her mouth. He might be as hungry as I was.

I opened the menu. While it came in a large brown folder, on the right was a hand-lettered page on cream paper. On the left was a narrow printed paper with the daily special.

Shim's always had two different steaks, some seafood, chicken, and a vegetarian meal. Tonight I was hungry. Unfortunately, the steaks were expensive and would blow my food budget for far too long, though I knew they were amazing. They had a seafood pasta on special that looked divine and was probably the source of the lovely garlic and basil I was smelling. If I got that, I could afford dessert if I were still hungry, particularly since I wasn't getting an alcoholic drink.

I closed the menu satisfied with my choice. The waitress came back and brought our drinks and a basket of assorted breads and rolls. Natalie ordered the smaller of the two steaks. Tyson got the same special I did. At least we'd both smell of garlic and basil, not that anything was likely to happen, I reminded myself.

"So, tell us what you learned from your investigator," Natalie said. If she stressed the word investigator a little much, Tyson didn't seem to notice. He reached in and started to grab for bread but then thought better of it, offering me a choice first. I took a sourdough roll. Natalie declined.

I buttered my roll as he began to talk.

"Everything she learned points to Trinity being at the café when Eric was murdered. The police don't have a definitive time of death, but Deborah talked to Millie Elkins, who works the main desk at the library. The cameras on the front show Trinity leaving before Eric's time of death, so unless she slipped in through the back entrance, she wasn't in the library," Tyson said.

"But a prosecutor could argue she went back," Natalie pressed.

I sunk my teeth into the soft bread of the roll, soothing my starving stomach. I couldn't remember the last time I'd eaten anything that tasted so good. I tried not to groan with joy as I chewed.

"The timing of when she arrived at the café doesn't work. Not only do we have Jade's estimate on the time, we have the time she paid for her drink on the credit card. Both Jade and Greg can testify that she didn't leave the café between then and your meeting. Your purchase is a few minutes later, so I assume you can verify that as well," Tyson said.

He looked at me specifically as he talked about the café. I hurriedly swallowed the bite I'd been chewing, hoping I didn't look too piggish, and nodded at him. "Greg's very honest and quite observant. I'm sure he even knew about what time Trinity arrived. Cade probably noticed as well."

Tyson pulled out a yellow legal pad and made a note on it.

"I've not been taking official statements yet because while she's being held and under arrest, I expect that we'll be able to get a judge to toss out the charges based on the information the police have. The chief has been helpful. The only reason they arrested her was because the mother of the young man who claims to have seen her murder Eric insisted."

"Fiona and Isaac McIvers and Mrs. Joyce Williamson," Natalie supplied.

"You got a name and you didn't tell me?" I demanded. I put a hand to my chest, not because I was being dramatic but I'd had to swallow a larger piece of bread than I wanted. I hoped that salads would come soon or I'd be rooting around in the breadbasket for another roll.

"I just found out after we talked," Natalie said easily. "I asked all the desk workers if they'd talked to her or gotten a name. I finally found someone who had. She had signed for room service the other day rather than Fiona."

I sipped my Dr. Pepper.

"Have you looked into them?" Natalie asked Tyson.

"So far as we can tell they've come here to research familiars. Fiona was having some trouble with her bird and decided that our library was the best place to search for help. We've got phone calls to our local veterinary clinic as well and the doctor there confirms that she's consulted with them," Tyson said. "She's not local so she's not actually a patient and bird familiars aren't always good with travel."

"Arizona is a long way," Natalie said. "Can you even bring birds on planes?"

No one knew exactly but it was a moot point as the bird was not actually here.

"We've confirmed Fiona's flight," Tyson said. "And that they did visit and consult with the vet when they were in town. They had a private session, sans familiar, and have spent time on the second floor of the library every day since they've been registered at the hotel."

"They aren't very well-liked," Natalie said.

"Isaac appears to be a problem child. The vet did say that he had concerns about Isaac with a familiar like a bird. He doesn't seem to have much impulse control and Fiona doesn't really discipline him. Apparently, they also looked at getting him his own familiar, but he hasn't bonded with any. Deborah talked to some Arizona locals and they say that Isaac has almost no magic and this is frustrating to Fiona. Given how she lets him get away with bad behavior, it seems like that's a good thing."

Our salads arrived and I dug into mine hungrily. The roll had helped but it was only enough to take the edge off. I considered grabbing another but I felt awkward being the only one chowing down.

"I can't sit here," a familiar voice said. "That woman is a terror."

I looked up to see Mrs. Ainsley pointing at me, in wicked Mrs. Ainsley mode. "She practically cursed me when I was in the café earlier. If I were you, I wouldn't allow such people in your restaurant!"

The hostess looked horrified. Tyson stood up and drew himself to his full height. I felt magic building around him, a silence spell to allow him to speak freely with Mrs. Ainsley.

"Jade Owlens is a respected member and business owner in our community. Your words could be considered slander. As an attorney and therefore an officer of the court, I'd ask you to consider your words. Anything further said about curses and magic will be reported to the council," Tyson said, staring directly at Mrs. Ainsley.

"As if that bothers me. Do you know how many council members are friends of mine? Don't even consider it. I'll throw magic where I will, when I will. And if you try and stop me, you'll regret it."

The hostess was now looking very pale and glancing around. The other diners didn't appear to notice anything when I looked back, which was good. Tyson's spell was holding.

Mrs. Ainsley stood there staring at him. Tyson didn't back down. I gripped the side of the table hoping someone would come and intervene.

atching Mrs. Ainsley and Tyson stare at each other with eyes hard and muscles tensed for magic sent chills down my spine. My knuckles turned white where I gripped the edge of the table. My heart hammered. I couldn't believe how Tyson had stood up for me. However, if he'd done nothing, perhaps Mrs. Ainsley would have gone away. Now she was in a stare-down with him.

Natalie sat equally still. I couldn't even tell if she was breathing.

Finally, Mrs. Ainsley spoke, "Young man, I have no idea what you want. Were you offering your table?" Her entire voice had changed. She was the nice elderly woman I'd first met and rather liked.

Still, watching, I noted her eyes flicked to me and away, without any recognition of what had just happened.

"Is it crowded today?" she asked. "I'd really like a more private table. People my age don't always eat as neatly as others and I'd rather not disturb someone," she said to the hostess.

The poor young woman let her breath out and led Mrs. Ainsley back to another part of the restaurant. She glanced back at our table twice to be sure we were okay. I had no doubt we'd soon be getting a visit from the manager making sure we were all okay.

Tyson sat down frowning. "Something's going on with her. I don't like it. The two people with her seemed to act as if this was normal and while she might have been suffering from this for some time, it's most definitely not normal. I'll have to report her to the council."

"The police probably already did that after I had to call for help at the café," I said.

"I heard about that," Tyson added. He paused to replace the white cloth napkin across his lap and looked longingly at his salad. He picked up the fork and put it down and picked it up again, clearly not sure whether to eat or talk.

I picked up my fork and dug into my salad. My stomach wasn't going to wait any longer for food.

"I cannot believe her. And I comped her room to get rid of her without a fuss," Natalie said. "I should have kicked her out tonight."

"Better she's there. The council can send someone to find her in the morning," Tyson said. "It won't take long to send someone from their Louisville office."

Natalie nodded. "If they're not already on their way."

"I should contact them about the McIvers, too," Tyson said, thoughtfully. He picked at his salad. "See if anyone has complained about them before."

It was pretty normal for businesses to check with the council about any witch they might be considering hiring so it wasn't like Tyson would be bringing undue notice to Fiona. I quickly forked plenty of lettuce, onion, and shredded carrots into my mouth. I was too hungry for the upset with Mrs. Ainsley to take away my appetite.

Natalie and Tyson ate much more slowly than I did. At this point, I didn't care. I needed food.

"Good idea," Natalie said, carrying on the conversation with Tyson. "What else do we know about that morning?"

"We know that Eric was upset about a missing book," Tyson told her. "A specialty breeding book that hasn't been used in years."

"I heard it was about creating familiars from ordinary animals," Natalie said.

Tyson nodded. "He yelled at Trinity. Several other library workers heard him. They don't all have permission to go into the archives. Trinity is the only person besides Eric who can go in there."

"What about someone from the outside?" Natalie asked. "Could they have broken in?"

"We're looking into that. If they did, they were good. The archives have computerized locks as well as magical protections. Of course, the magic mostly just keeps out those who don't belong and it's hard to know what the intent was when it was set," Tyson said.

Broad spells against anyone who doesn't belong tend to fairly useless. Unless you had a specific person, like, say, Mrs. Ainsley, those had no real value. It depended upon the person trying to enter feeling as if they didn't belong. A good thief might feel perfectly fine walking in someplace they didn't belong. A legitimate person entering might be suffering from some imposter syndrome and set off the alarm.

"What about the computer surveillance?" Natalie asked. She shrugged off the spell, while she took a dainty bite of the salad.

Tyson shoveled a bit of his own salad into his mouth. While he'd been off his dinner for a few moments after Mrs. Ainsley came by, he was back to eating almost as much as I was. His work may have kept him from having lunch.

"The only thing that Deborah found that's suspicious is a slight glitch shortly after closing the night before. It's possible that a thief hacked into the system and covered their tracks, but it wasn't perfectly done. If Deborah's company didn't have such good computer people, no one would have noticed the glitch in the images."

Tyson frowned a little and shook his head. "This is way bigger than Trinity. I'm fairly certain I can get the charges dropped, but it would be so much easier if we had a real suspect. Worse, what if Eric's not the only person the killer is after?"

Natalie choked on the half piece of lettuce she had just started to chew. Fortunately, I was only mopping up the last of my blue cheese dressing, trying to decide if I wanted another roll.

"You think?" I asked when Natalie was too busy coughing to say anything.

"We don't know why they took that book. I do know that it has magic forbidden by the council. I only found out about it when I inquired about the book thinking it was a lead. Maybe it is," Tyson said. "It's in archives because it can only be read by those with council permission which means it shouldn't go out of the archival reading rooms."

"Do you think the person who took the book is connected to Eric's murder?" I asked.

"That I don't know," Tyson said. "It seems too coincidental otherwise. It's not like the library has books stolen on a regular basis. Misplaced by patrons now and then, but archival volumes rarely have issues. The timing..."

I nodded.

"Is too much," Natalie said. "I wonder if there was something in there that Fiona thought would help her familiar?"

"I can't see how," I said. "Not if it's just about changing an ordinary creature into a familiar."

"I was thinking transferring intellects from one body to another or something. Maybe she wants to get her bird a new body?"

Tyson smiled a little.

"What?" Natalie asked. "They do it in the movies all the time, even for ordinary people."

Our main courses arrived. The manager brought them and after serving us, he apologized for Mrs. Ainsley and comped our meals, and offered a free dessert. The one good thing to come out of all the nasty people in town that I'd been running into was that I was getting all sorts of special accommodations at our local restaurants. I'd have to remember to return the favor when they came into the café, not that my coffees and teas were anywhere near the same level of value as their meals.

"But it's not something you can do from familiar to familiar. If you could, we'd be seeing witches putting their dying familiar's souls into other bodies all the time. Or at least they would if they were negative magic practitioners," Tyson said.

"It would be nice if we could," Natalie said sadly. Her first two familiars had been rats. And while they lived longer than ordinary rats, they had still died after only a few years. In both cases, Natalie had been heartbroken. She'd been reluctant to choose a different familiar, but eventually, she'd bonded with LaRue after being without a familiar for several years.

"Think about how many ordinary animals would die," Tyson said quietly. He took a bite of his pasta and half-closed his eyes.

Natalie cut some of her steak and looked at the pink inside. She pressed her fork against it, perhaps testing how rare it was—Natalie prefers her steak to practically moo—before taking a bite.

I ate my pasta. The discussion about familiars had quieted us all down and we ate in silence for a bit. I savored every bite, practically feeling my reserves building again as I ate. I should have eaten more after my spell work earlier. It'd been foolish to think I could wait until dinner. I'd have been starving even if I hadn't had to wait on Natalie.

As we finished and I perused the dessert menu, thankful that the meal was being comped and I had an excuse, Natalie went back to talking about Trinity's case.

"I just don't get why Isaac would have focused on her," Natalie said. "Or why someone would want to set her up."

"If they did," I said, setting the small dessert card down having decided upon a five-layer chocolate cake, "they didn't know our schedule very well. Most locals do."

"That's a good point," Tyson said making a note on the pad of paper he'd shoved aside. He gave me a big smile.

I smiled right back. It seemed like he held my gaze a bit longer than was comfortable, but I was probably just reading something into things. Still, I felt tingly enough that I worried someone had spiked my Dr. Pepper.

"But why Trinity?" Natalie said again.

The waitress came back. Natalie got another wine spritzer. I got some tea and the cake. Tyson got decaf coffee and a piece of the tiramisu.

"I haven't a clue," Tyson said. "If Trinity has any ideas she hasn't given them to me."

"Maybe because the murderer knew about the book and knew enough about the library to realize Trinity was the only other person with access to the archives?" I asked.

"Most likely," Tyson said. "But then we're back looking for a thief."

"A thief who has an ordinary pet they want to bond with," Natalie said.

"Or a familiar who has lost their magic somehow?" I suggested. It wasn't impossible for familiars to lose their magic. It was particularly true if someone used negative magic and the familiar wasn't comfortable doing so. They can't not help their witch. In the emotional turmoil of wanting to avoid doing harm and obeying their witch, the magic can disappear.

"That's a different issue," Natalie said.

"Actually, a few years back I had an interesting case," Tyson said. "The witch purchased a puppy from a breeder who said it had tested as a familiar. The witch had fallen in love, but as the pup grew they didn't manifest any magic. The witch sued the breeder for lying to them. As it turned out, this particular breeder would just sell all the pups from their litters as familiars even though they wouldn't all end up being magical. They were counting on the people being so bonded to the dogs that they wouldn't complain. Naturally, that didn't last long."

"No matter how bonded you are, you want what you paid for," Natalie said. "I suppose they expected that the threat of losing the dog was enough."

"Exactly," Tyson said nodding. He smiled at her but I was certain it wasn't for quite as long as he smiled at me.

I bit my lip thinking. "It's possible they knew that Trinity and I were friends. Could they think one of my cats wasn't magical?"

"But all of your cats are magical," Natalie said.

"People search for familiars all over," I told her. "They could have gotten a cat elsewhere when it turned out it wasn't a familiar and thought they got it from me. Or they got it from someone who said it was from me even though it wasn't."

"The last I could believe, except you say that you'll take back any familiar that doesn't work out, don't you?" Natalie asked.

I nodded. "I doubt everyone pays attention to that part, though."

"Especially if they didn't actually visit with you," Tyson added. He made a note on the yellow legal pad that he'd kept out on the table. "And, the original person could have gotten it from the shelter and saw your café name and thought that you'd taken over the entire shelter, too."

The waitress came back with our drinks and told us the dessert would be out shortly.

I finally felt able to wait for food though I had plenty of room for some cake, at least I hoped so. If I couldn't finish, I was definitely taking the rest home.

When the cake came, I made a comment about all the irritable people in town and how I needed the cake.

"Someone besides Fiona and Isaac and that Mrs. Ainsley?" Tyson asked.

I told him about Flori and her friends and how difficult she'd been. "While it happened after Eric died, Trinity wasn't arrested yet. It's like Flori was the one who put a curse on me and she didn't even realize it," I said.

Tyson made a note.

"That was a joke," I reminded him.

"But it's interesting timing. Aren't most of your customers pretty easy-going? People you like?"

"Generally, but it's not like I like everyone," I said. "I'm sure there are always weeks when there are more difficult people than other weeks. We just noticed it this week because of Trinity."

"Did you report Flori?" Tyson asked.

I nodded. "I did. I even got a confirmation about my report and asking for additional information from the council the next day. I mean, I didn't have any, but they asked."

"Good," Tyson said. "Someone probably visited the shop already and found her. I'll send them a note to ask about her as well. If this doesn't get tossed out, I'll want anyone who could possibly have anything to do with the case found. If I had a way of figuring out the names of every person who set foot in town that day, I'd use it."

"Your detective can probably find some information on the hotel records," Natalie said sweetly. "I can't give out that information unless you have a warrant or something like that, but I bet she knows someone who could figure out a way to get the information if they know it's there."

Tyson gave a tight smile but said nothing. He took a bite of his tiramisu and nodded. "This is good."

That changed the subject to food, again. I was just fine as I ate away at my chocolate cake. Natalie even took a small bite, but just a single tiny bite. She always says she's watching her figure.

I didn't say anything but I wondered if Tyson's refusal to answer Natalie meant that Deborah's company had already been fishing in Natalie's computer records. And I wondered if they'd found anything that would turn out to be useful.

24

By the time Natalie dropped me back at my apartment, I was fading into a food coma. I wanted nothing so much as a hot bath and to head off to bed. Saturdays were busy at the café and I was in early, along with Charlene and Jason. Jason only worked weekends. He worked all day Saturday and half-days on Sunday.

Mason greeted me, twinging around my legs. "No problems?" I asked, dropping my purse down. I hardly paused.

Mason had to trot to catch up and give me any updates. Nothing had happened. All was still okay down in the café.

"I'm not surprised," I said. "Mrs. Ainsley was at Shim's."

Did you bring me steak? Mason asked. I'd made the mistake of once bringing home a little steak for him. Now he always wanted it.

"I had seafood pasta and it had all sorts of spices that are bad for cats." I tossed my clothing into the laundry bag in the bedroom so I could take a quick shower. I still felt hot and icky after the day I'd had. The warm water would help me relax.

I felt someone around the protections, Mason said. *They attempted to get inside but couldn't. It was fairly bold.*

"Do we need to do anything?" I asked.

Mason leaped on the bathroom counter and I laid a hand on his side so we could communicate. *At this point, no.*

"Good."

I went over to the shower to turn on the water. I closed my eyes as it warmed up. I couldn't wait for it to pound on my back and my head. Showering now meant I could sleep an extra few minutes in the morning. That was a huge perk.

Mason kept watch while I went about cleaning up and trying to relax. I didn't stay in as long as I might have wanted because I was exhausted. I barely got my hair mostly dry with the blow dryer before I was falling into bed, asleep before I'd pulled the covers over me.

I heard nothing until about an hour before my alarm was due to go off. Mason woke me with his howls.

Light from the parking area seeps through the slats in the blinds on the window so it wasn't completely dark in my bedroom. It's not a large room but big enough. Mason wasn't on the bed. He was out in the main part of the apartment.

I shot up out of bed and tossed off the covers. I didn't even think about being dressed only in my flimsy shorts and t-shirt pajamas that I wear nor did I care that I was barefoot. In fact, I didn't even feel the chill of the floor, which always seems cool, even in the summer.

I'd not closed the blinds in the main living area so the lights from the street made the room almost as bright as if I had the overhead fixture on. Mason was near the exterior door making a racket. He leaned back on his hind legs and pawed at the wood, looking around, howling at the top of his lungs.

I ran over to him and touched his head.

Someone's trying to get in downstairs. Mischief, Mason said.

I hurriedly found some shoes, grabbed my phone, which I'd plugged in on the kitchen counter, and went out. I didn't take Mason, lest he insist upon protecting the familiars in the café at the expense of his own safety.

He was grumbling even as I closed the door practically on his pink nose.

I ran down the stairs and slipped into the café through the back door. The cats down there were meowing, loudly. I hadn't ever heard them all in chorus and certainly not when I first came down. I debated and then flipped on the light in the back room. Everyone was at the front of the kennels, even Jelliane who almost never pressed against the bars.

Too bad I had been so protective of Mason. His telepathy might have given me an idea of what I was up against.

I found the number for the police department. I could have called 911 but the emergency number was routed through the county and what would they say to a woman upset because her cats were distressed? They'd laugh. No, I needed a witch, and the best way to get one was to call the department directly.

"Waverton Police Department," a male voice said. I didn't recognize it. Still, if you worked for the Waverton Police Department, you had to be a witch.

"This is Jade Owlens," I said. "I'm at the familiar café on Park Street. Something is going on. The familiars are all up in arms. I have a new protection spell on the place and I think that warned my familiar as well."

"We'll send someone out," the voice said. "Where are you?"

"I'm in the back room with the cats," I said. I kept my voice low. I tried looking out through the door to the cat area of the café, but saw nothing. It seemed darker out there.

"Stay there," the person said. "If someone has broken in, you could be hurt."

"No one should have been able to break in," I said. "The protection spell…"

"It happens," the male cut me off.

Of *course* it happens. I knew that, but I'd just renewed the darned spell. People got through protection spells on property because the spells were getting weak. Spells last for years but not forever. The level of magic needed to get through a freshly laid spell by two people and a familiar, not to mention the older spells I had to protect my apartment, would be huge.

It wouldn't do any good to argue with the dispatcher. I'd have to do it with whoever answered the call if it became an issue. I strained my ears to hear something, but the cats were making too much noise.

I sniffed the air, but someone had used the litter box so I couldn't even tell if the smell of the place was off.

Fear made me shiver in my short pajamas. Except that as I rubbed my arms, still holding my phone but using my wrist, I felt cold. Goosebumps rose. I got more chilled.

Something was very wrong. Negative magic could lower temperature. So could a spirit. The cats started screaming and howling, though I saw nothing. Cats had far better senses about ghosts and spirits and I had no doubt they could see whatever was moving around.

"I think someone has called up a spirit," I whispered into the phone. I hoped that if there was something that it hadn't broken my phone connection. Non-corporeal entities could do that.

"I'll let them know," the man on the other end of the phone said quietly. His voice had taken on a more serious tone. Spirits were nothing to mess with.

I heard car doors slamming outside. Red and blue lights created odd shapes on the cat room beyond the closed door.

I hurried out to the main room, noting that the chairs

were still where they'd been when I'd left last night. In the main café area, everything looked as if it were in place. The officers banged on the door. A spirit would have set off the protection spells and should have been kept out, but it wouldn't need the door.

I unlocked it.

Two officers I didn't know came in. One was an older man with gray hair and a weathered face. The other was a much younger man with a shaven head.

They shivered coming in. I was still shaking. The cats were still howling.

The men barely glanced at me before hurrying to the back. The familiars were upset and scared. If this was an attack with a spirit, they were the focus.

I closed the door, debating about locking it. I was still doing that when I noted a shadow running up to the door. I turned the lock. The shadow banged at it. It took me a moment to realize it was a figure in a hooded sweatshirt, all in black. Their hands banged on the glass, pressing against it, trying to get in.

I backed up, staring at whoever it was. The hood fell back. Flori looked in, but her eyes were different. Gone was the color that had been in them. Now, they were solid black, the color practically eating away at the whites.

She didn't appear to see me.

I put a hand over my mouth as she continued to pound on the glass.

I felt the officers in the back doing a containment spell. The cats began to quiet. Though they were still meowing, the sounds no longer held the terror and frustration of earlier. I'd have to bring Mason down to help calm them further and to let me know what they needed.

The chill left my body as suddenly as it came on. Flori dropped from the glass on the door to the ground just as that happened. I walked a few tentative steps to the door, looking out through the glass, half expecting her to leap up and begin pounding. Instead, I saw her there, crumpled against the locked door, so still I wasn't sure she was breathing.

"We have your spirit," the older officer said.

I looked at him and pointed to the door. He handed over a spirit catcher box to the younger officer and looked out at Flori.

He turned back to me puzzled. I shrugged. I backed up while he opened the door, prepared to let him defend the café if Flori suddenly rose up and tried to dash inside.

Flori didn't move. With the door open, I noted that she was wearing a blue jean skirt and heavy black boots. She had on a stretched-out green t-shirt, not tucked in. She looked as if she'd been sleeping in her clothing for some time. Except that she'd been in the café just a few days before and I didn't remember that outfit.

"You know this woman?" the older officer asked. I noted a name on the name tag said David Halvorson.

"She came into the café the other day with several friends. I think there were six of them. I tried to picture the group to see what I recalled. "They were all ordinaries. She had magic. In fact, I called the council because she didn't seem to know she had magic."

Officer Halvorson looked up moments before I heard someone walking down the street. Not a heel tap so much as that a swish of fabric and a periodic squish of a soft-soled shoe.

I looked to my left and saw two women walking towards us, striding purposefully. They were in blue jeans and t-shirts. The bottle blonde had a jean jacket on. The red-head had her arms bare to the night.

"So this is Flori," the redhead said. She pulled a wallet from a front pocket and showed us a badge. It leaked council magic, letting me know she was from the WBI.

"She released a spirit," Officer Halvorson said. He gave the two women a long look that asked where they had been when my café was being attacked.

"No, actually she didn't," the red-haired woman said. "I felt the calling and it didn't come from her. It's why she got so close to the café before we did. We were trying to get a fix on the calling."

The blonde looked around. "I'm not sure the spirit was dead, either."

"What do you mean?" I asked. It wasn't like you just called up a spirit from a living person. People's spirits didn't just get up and walk out of their bodies, not, I mean, unless they'd just died.

The blonde stared at me. Her eyes were extraordinarily pale. Maybe her short white hair wasn't from a bottle. Maybe she was really that pale.

The light around the café didn't help. It bleaches out the best of us. Even the redhead didn't look as vibrant as I had a feeling she normally did, her hair slightly lank around her shoulders.

"I think someone knowingly pulled a spirit from one body and was attempting to put it in another," the blonde said.

"You can do that?" I asked. Stupid question. If you had enough power and no conscience you could do practically anything. Wasn't that just what Natalie, Tyson, and I had talked about in regards to familiars the other night?

The blonde cocked her head. "In theory."

So no one actually knew if it could be done.

"My guess is that this is the spirit that was called, but why was it called here?" Red asked.

"I've had some trouble at the café," I supplied. "An old woman, a Mrs. Ainsley, was quite angry with me. She threatened the café."

"Hence the new protection spell," Red-hair said. "It's strong. And well-woven. I sense a feline familiar?"

I nodded.

"It wasn't you alone, though. Your partner works well with you."

"Thanks. He's one of my employees," I said. I'd tell Greg what the councilwoman said. I wasn't sure whether being praised by them was a good thing or not. They did know good magic, though, so there was that.

Red nodded and then looked at Flori. The two women gathered her up, trying to make her walk. Flori stumbled along as if she were drunk. After a couple of steps, the two set her down, leaning her back against the café.

"We'll need the spirit box," Red said.

Officer Halvorson looked a bit uncertain.

Red fingered her pocket as she was planning to pull out the badge again, reminding him. Halvorson handed it over.

"I still need to report what happened," he said. "We've got some un-attached familiars in there quite upset. They could have been hurt."

The blonde frowned. "Interesting. And you had someone threaten you earlier? Was it reported?"

I nodded.

The blonde half closed her eyes and put a hand in her pocket. I got the impression the badges let her communicate with the rest of the council. When she opened them she looked at me. "Do you know of any connection between this girl and the old woman?"

I shook my head. "Flori, that's what her friends called the

girl, and her friends came in shortly after Mrs. Ainsley. So they passed each other in the café, but they didn't seem to know each other."

The blonde nodded. "We'll get her to Waverton's clinic and take care of her there. We might have more questions for you later."

"I'll be here," I said. The night looked a bit lighter than it had earlier. I went back inside.

"I need to go up and get dressed for work," I said. "Is that okay?"

"It looks like it's just your familiars that are upset," Halvorson said. The cats were still mewing but it had moved down a notch from earlier. Now it was mostly mews and mrrps. The younger officer came out from the back.

"I double-checked all of them and I couldn't find any spells on them," he said. Then he nodded at me. "I'm pretty good at that sort of thing."

"And they seem okay? Nothing is going to cause problems later? I have a busy Saturday for the familiars. Plenty of visitors."

If there was a potential problem, I could probably call a few breeders who would be willing to socialize some kittens over the weekend. Most kittens would be spoken for if they turned out to be magical, but at least I'd have cats for the visitors to spend time with.

"I think everything's fine. Have your familiar check, though," the young officer told me. He had himself angled away like he couldn't wait to get out of the café so I didn't catch his name. As I locked up after the two men, I realized he'd likely been in a hurry because he was probably about off shift. Nothing personal.

I hurried upstairs to change clothes, get Mason, and start the day. I already felt as if I'd had a full day and it hadn't even begun!

I got ready in record time. I am not normally a woman who takes a ton of time to fix her hair and such, but today I hurried even through my minimal morning routine. I thanked heavens for the fact that I'd been so fatigued last night that I'd already showered. When I got Mason in his carrier to take downstairs, I was breathing hard.

It didn't help that Mason had twined about my legs trying to pick up everything I knew about what had happened. He was annoyed that I hadn't brought him down, though he did admit that, of course, he would have risked his life for the familiars. They were in his territory as honored guests. It was only right.

Perhaps that's the way feline familiars saw the world but it wasn't the way witches like me saw the world. I needed to protect him most of all. I'd have felt awful if I'd have lost one of the café cats, but it wouldn't hold a candle to how I'd feel if I lost Mason.

Once inside the cafe, I let Mason out and then the other

familiars. They all crowded around him. I felt the calming spell he did to make sure that they were all going to be okay. I spent some time checking eyes and ears and paw pads. It allowed me to feel their fur. Most of them felt a bit too silky soft which was an indication, to my fingers, that they'd been stressed. I considered calling a few of the breeders to get kittens or even their adults just for show but then decided against it.

Mason seemed to have things well in hand with the familiars he knew. New cats, cats he didn't know well, would take him a bit of time to get used to and probably create more stress on him.

While I cleaned the cages, I did small spells to search for anything magical that the spirit might have left behind that could harm one of the cats. I found nothing. A single cold spot lingered near Jelliane's kennel, but a small wind spell sent it off to the closet where it dissipated a few minutes later.

I found nothing else.

Jason got in before I'd even finished. His boyish-round face showed surprise to see me still working. That's one thing about Jason. He wasn't my youngest worker, but you could always tell what he was thinking. I think that, and his pale blonde hair, gave him a particularly youthful appearance. I gave him a brief overview of what had happened.

"That's just weird," he said. He hurried to the front to get things started for the day. He looked back at me a few times as if he had more to say, but knew there wasn't much time for it. Our customers would be there soon enough.

I got dry food out, finished the litterboxes, and took one final look around the feline room. Nothing was out of order except a single book knocked off one of the tables. It was a cozy mystery novel by a local author. I set it back on the table frowning. It hadn't been there last night. Perhaps the ghost or spirit or whatever had tried to move things and the book was the only thing it had succeeded with.

The book was a cute mystery about a quilter in Montana. Nothing I'd learned linked quilting with the other mysteries, so I doubted it was a clue. I filed the out-of-place item away in my mind as I went to the front counter to finish helping Jason set up. I noticed he'd gotten all the chairs down off the tables and was taking notes to fill the front cooler.

I wiped down all the machines and made sure the front refrigerator was full of milk. I double-checked our flavorings so that I wouldn't have to change anything out during a rush. Charlene arrived just as I unlocked the front door and turned the sign from closed to open. She was quickly followed by two Saturday regular customers.

I let Jason pull drinks this morning while I got the register. He would be faster than I was considering how little sleep I'd gotten.

"So what got you here so early?" Jason asked. Clearly, his curiosity had gotten the better of him, though he'd tried to rein it in. I liked that he tried to mind his own business, but that he cared enough to ask.

"I got an alarm from down here about an hour before I was due to get up." I told him about the spirit and about Flori falling down in front of the building.

"Maybe someone called her spirit out to get into this place. She thinks she's ordinary but she's a witch, right?" Jason asked after I told him all about Flori and who she was. Charlene wiped down the front, clearly listening in.

I nodded and told him more about the WBI witches. We had a customer come in so that paused our discussion. I rang up the woman and Jason got her coffee. Charlene hurried around to heat up a pastry for her.

Three more people came in, preventing us from continuing our discussion. Our first familiar visitors arrived and while they ordered, Charlene went in to be sure the room was in order and the cats ready for company.

After that, our Saturday morning rush began. Charlene and I rang up people while Jason made drinks. Charlene got regular drinks. The morning flew by and pretty soon it was time for lunch breaks.

I sent Jason off first as he'd arrived earlier. Charlene took over on the drinks and I remained on the register. I also helped get visitors to the familiar room settled. Everyone seemed pleasant enough for which I was grateful. I was a little surprised that I hadn't heard much gossip about my early morning alarm.

"The cats seem less settled than usual," Charlene observed after doing a quick clean between visitors to the feline room. "It was probably the break-in."

I nodded, agreeing. "I can't believe it, though. Greg and I did a protection spell yesterday. Can you imagine the power?"

Charlene shook her head. "That's so strange. And that poor girl outside," she said.

"She wasn't the nicest witch I've ever met, but she was untrained." I noticed a drop of milk on the counter and wiped it off, while Charlene looked thoughtful.

"Could someone be trying to take over her spirit, but she was trying to get away?" Charlene asking. "An untrained witch with the power you've said Flori had would be quite a find for an unscrupulous person. The first time, she wouldn't have had a clue and they could have made her do anything. I mean, it's not easy to move items and certainly not far, but maybe they got her to move that book in the library, just outside the archives? This time, they tried to get her to do something else and the poor girl fought back."

"Could she have murdered Eric?" I asked.

Charlene shrugged. "Spirits do have a bit of ability. My

dad worked on some cases but nothing like a murder. For instance, they might be able to open kennel doors but probably couldn't move one of the cats further than the floor. They could have surprised Eric into falling down the stairs, but didn't I hear he was beaten to death?"

I told her he was.

If Flori's spirit had managed to move the book out of the archives and hidden it in the regular stacks, anyone could have stolen it, if they knew where to look. Could she have opened the locked door though? Of course, it wouldn't have had locks from the inside. That was a potential safety issue.

"Stealing the book would certainly be possible for a spirit. Even just getting it out of the archives. Of course, if Eric did a locator spell earlier than expected, it should have been found." Charlene was clearly thinking out loud. "Unless someone put a major spell on the book to hide it from the locator spell."

"I think Trinity mentioned that Eric did a locator spell to find the book," I said. "Of course, what if Eric was the one trying to steal the book and he wanted to point a finger at Trinity?"

Charlene shrugged. "My dad says mysteries are usually straightforward. Of course, sometimes you have to see the forest in amongst all the trees for it to really make sense."

It was certainly possible that I had too much information. It would be like working a puzzle with extra pieces and you didn't know which ones didn't fit. I bit my lip and took the next order when a group of people came through the door. I knew them slightly and we all chatted about the weather and made nice. In amongst themselves, they talked about Eric, stealing glances over at me.

I'd be glad when Eric's killer had been arrested and people would stop acting like they were in the presence of a criminal mastermind. I hadn't even done anything except have one of my best friends arrested on the eyewitness account of a child. A not-very-reliable child, too, from everything I'd heard.

It was interesting that Isaac's mother was so insistent that he be believed when, as far as I knew, she hadn't seen anything. They were in the special library where children weren't supposed to be unattended. I wondered how Isaac could have been in a place to see the murder, when Fiona didn't see anything. Now that I thought about it, he hadn't been on the steps with her when she was crying, at least not that I could remember.

At some point, I ought to make sure Tyson remembered that children weren't supposed to be unattended. And Isaac was the sort of child who really needed to be watched.

When Jason got back from lunch, I sent Tyson a quick text. I was still waiting for a response when I headed out the back to go upstairs and grab a bite for lunch.

Outside, I smelled smoke. Before I had even let the back-door close, I heard sirens coming closer, quickly followed by the long, low honk of a fire engine. I went back through the door and through the café so I could look out the front. I had to push my way past a few people who had also heard the sounds and had the same idea. The engine passed the café, much to my relief, not that a fire would start easily with the protection spells I had on it.

I stepped outside and immediately smelled smoke. Gray clouds of it came from my right, not far down the street.

I hurried in that direction with a group of people who had been downtown. My stomach sank as I realized the smoke was coming from Sarah Meyerson's bookstore.

2 7

I wasn't the only one gawking at the smoke. Just as when Eric was murdered and the police had been cordoning off the street, most of the people who had been wandering around or working had come out to see what was going on. I worried about Peggy's parrot rescue next door. No doubt she had plenty of protection spells, but birds are sensitive. Like me, Peggy would never forgive herself if something happened to one of those birds.

I didn't see any flames. While that felt like good news to me, the less good news was that I didn't see Sarah out amongst the people watching. She was always at her store. Like me, she was a small business owner and spent a great deal of time there even when employees might be covering for her. Someone was cuddling Shayla, so at least the book-store cat was safe.

Unlike me, Sarah didn't live upstairs. Her landlord had rented that space out to a group of therapists who were willing to work on the second floor, though he'd been required to install an elevator. I hoped that no one had an appointment today

While the weather remained hot and humid I rubbed my arms, suddenly chilled. First Eric and a missing archival book and now Sarah's bookstore. The mysteries going on clearly centered around books. Even the one thing out of place in my café this morning had been a book. I frowned.

So far as I knew, Sarah's store didn't carry anything too exotic. In fact, it was one of the reasons Eric had criticized her. I bit my lip as I watched.

I wish I knew more about the book in the archives. Trinity might know. In fact, if Trinity did know what was in it, then suddenly her being accused of a murder she didn't commit made sense. I tried to push my way through the crowd to get to Tyson's but I couldn't get through.

The sidewalk outside the bookstore was blocked off and Tyson's office was beyond the bookstore. I turned and went back to the café. It was easier going that way because people were eager to push closer to each other to see what was going on.

I heard people whispering about Sarah. Most sounded worried for her. Someone had started a rumor that she was in the store and no one had heard from her since. I did hear that her morning employee had gotten out.

I tried not to worry about Sarah too much. Just because she wasn't answering her phone meant nothing. If the café was burning, it wasn't likely I'd be answering my phone either, no matter if I and all the familiars were out and safe. In fact, in getting the familiars to safety, it's very likely I'd have forgotten all about my phone. I hoped Sarah was the same way.

No crowds waited outside my business. A few people were inside, getting drinks. Charlene and Jason were serving. Jason looked up surprised to see me.

"I got distracted," I said. I pulled out my phone and headed to the back. It was quieter there and I didn't really want anyone to overhear my conversation. My route took me through the familiar room.

A beautiful dark-haired woman sat in a chair with Jelliane quietly petting her. Kitika was on the back of the woman's chair. Two other cats were near her feet, snoozing. I raised an eyebrow.

Her companion, a tall, thin man with equally dark hair and skin only a few shades lighter, sat in the chair next to her, which was one of my favorites. Mason snoozed on his lap. The man smiled at me.

"Cats love her," he said, looking over fondly at the woman. Clearly, the cats weren't the only ones who did.

I smiled back, enjoying the moment. I reached out a tendril of magic. She was ordinary. Perhaps just someone who enjoyed visiting cat cafes because of a love of cats.

I went through the door to the back and leaned against the far wall. I called Tyson's office. No answer. Saturday. There wouldn't be.

I had called Tyson's personal number feeling my palms start to sweat as it rang through. I had already texted him once that day.

"Jade!" Tyson's voice sounded surprised, and, I hoped, rather happy.

"Did you hear about Sarah Meyerson's bookstore?" I asked, not bothering with a greeting.

"Just a few minutes ago." Now he sounded puzzled.

"I was thinking that this is the second time a crime has involved books. I was wishing I knew what was in the missing archive book from the special library. I figured Trinity would know. What if that's the reason whoever killed Eric made it look like it was her? What if Trinity knows what's in the book and that will give us an idea of who we're looking for?"

Tyson didn't say anything for a moment. I wondered if he thought I was insane.

"Trinity mentioned the book and she knows generally what it's about but I can't imagine that there's something that she knows…" he was thoughtful.

"What if someone thinks she knows something?" I asked.

"That's more likely," he said. "You're reading an awful lot into a fire at Sarah's, though."

"Do you really believe this is all coincidence?" I demanded. Waverton didn't have that much crime. We weren't a perfect little town and witch crime can get out of hand, but we normally didn't have a run of major incidents like this.

"Unlikely," Tyson said. "I was thinking it was more likely that whoever stole the book from the library didn't find what they wanted. My thought was that they talked to Sarah about a book that has since gone missing and they're hoping the fire will keep her from noticing. Trinity could easily have been a target of opportunity. They saw her with Eric regularly and figured that using magic to look like her would keep them from being suspects."

"That's true," I said. "You said the book was about making ordinary animals into familiars. It's not something that's done. What kind of book would Sarah have gotten that had anything to do with that?"

"That's a question for Deborah to research," Tyson said quietly. "Given that this person isn't above trying to break into your café—and yes I heard about that, too—I think you need to lay low and concentrate on your business. Deborah is trained to handle a witch coming after her. She doesn't have a café full of familiars who could be harmed if someone got past her protections, either, spirit or otherwise."

He was right and I hated it. "That was Flori, I think," I said. "The WBI had people watching her."

"I heard," Tyson said.

"Did they mention where they thought she got her magic?" I asked.

"That I haven't heard," Tyson said. "I do know they're staying at the hotel, though, if you want to go ask."

I heard the slightest hint of laughter in his voice. You didn't normally go in and start asking questions of the council or the WBI, but this time, I needed answers. Too much was happening in town right now. Flori had to be involved. I didn't understand how, but maybe I could figure something out if I had a few more answers about her.

I knew I wouldn't get anywhere by sending an email or calling the main number. I'd have to drive over to the hotel and hope to find one of the witches in. Hopefully, Natalie would be working and could get me a room number. I really needed to find out what was going on.

Jason and Charlene would be good until I returned. Charlene normally got the slightly slower hours because she usually came in late in the day three days a week, but she was a hard worker. Jason needed the extra money working weekends brought in. I'd found him to be an efficient worker. He'd finish his studies at the college soon enough and I'd lose him, which would require hiring someone else, not something I was looking forward to.

I sighed, dreading having to do that, and took a final glance in at the cats in the feline room before leaving. I felt guilty about running my errand. It wasn't that I planned to be gone all afternoon. Chances were, I'd just be taking a longish lunch and that only if I stopped for food. My stomach growled reminding me I'd missed breakfast that morning, too.

The sun was bright, though I saw clouds coming in from the west. I had a feeling that by the time evening rolled around, we'd get a good thunderstorm, perhaps even some flash flood warnings. Waverton tended to be up high enough that we rarely had to worry about flooding, though in heavy rains our streets quickly became shallow streams of fast running water.

Natalie's hotel was on the east side of the town, closer to I-75, though it's a good half-hour drive to the interstate. The building is a long narrow rectangle that resembles every standard hotel chain in the United States. It's painted cream with brown trim and the sign is different. It stands five stories high, which is large for a small town. It's larger than many hotels just off the freeway, which surprised me the first time I'd traveled and was old enough to notice the difference. We have two bed and breakfasts in town for those who don't want to stay in a hotel. Around the corner from the hotel is a restaurant that serves a hearty, hot meal for guests who don't want to travel too far.

One wing of the main floor holds conference rooms. With a large flagstone patio out back, the rooms on that side are often used for weddings because of the view. It's not like the view at Shim's, but it's pleasant enough with the low rolling hills and the occasional wandering horse. Back when Lyn Upton got married, the first person I sort of knew who did, she'd held her wedding there and the sheep from the Puller familiar farm got out and went running across the hills ba-ing for all they were worth.

Naturally, this all happened just as Lyn and Wills were talking about loving, honoring, and cherishing. The photographer got a bunch of photos and those are pretty famous around town. I think Natalie even has a print in her wedding book for prospective brides. It allows her or her representative to make the sales pitch a little bit more homey and casual than the standard business pitch.

Locals don't need the pitch. We know there aren't many other places in town to get married, but sometimes we do get folks from out of town. Those folks need a sales pitch. As far as Natalie is concerned if they want to go elsewhere to avoid sheep running through a wedding, they can go. It's not like sheep go stampeding past a wedding on a regular basis.

Natalie recently had the interior of the hotel re-done. The blue carpet was replaced with luxury vinyl plank in a sort of gray-brown tone. It looked like wood, though I always thought I could feel the difference. From a magical perspective, there was a completely different energy.

The front desk sat back and off to the right, a large shiny black thing that came up to my chest. Natalie's workers had a little step on their side so they could more easily see over the tall counter. Behind the front desk was the door to Natalie's office.

Before I got to over there, I had to walk past two large flower arrangements that stood so tall and wide that I felt like I was in a primeval forest. I often joked with Natalie that she ought to get a fake dinosaur to peer out between the flowers. She laughs, but sometimes she looks a bit worried like she's afraid someone else might do it just to prank her. Someday, Trinity just might.

Once past the flowers, the going was clear, two seating areas with the chairs far enough away that a family of four or more could easily walk next to each other, all with their luggage being carried in one of the luggage carts. There were no flowers anywhere else in the lobby, which was good considering how overboard the ones near the door were.

Several men dressed in shorts and t-shirts hurried out of the hotel. A mother and a young girl walked in just about the time the men left. I couldn't quite hear the conversations, though I knew they were having them.

The elevators were straight ahead, in a little alcove just beyond the desk. They were close enough that the desk worker could easily see who was going upstairs, but they were also visible to the people coming in so they weren't having to ask the front desk where the elevators were. To the far left was a large staircase that wound up to the second floor, which had a nice mezzanine with more chairs and a couple of tables where people could sit and look out over the lobby if they had nothing better to do. Natalie often talked about how it made her feel spied upon.

Natalie wasn't at the front desk, but I went up there and asked for her. She came out of the office before I'd even had a chance to finish her name, probably listening to what was going on.

"What brings you here?" she asked, looking me up and down.

I glanced at the girl at the front counter who had been about to say something. She was young and blonde and looked vaguely familiar, though I couldn't place her. She was probably related to someone I did know, though.

"Let's go someplace private," Natalie said, clearly aware that I didn't want to talk in front of someone I didn't know. She walked around the side of the desk and through a door that blended into the wall so well that it was easy to overlook. She took my arm and walked me back out of the hotel. I had hoped to talk in her office. That way she'd have her computer right at hand.

"It's about Trinity," I said quietly.

No one suddenly appeared and stared at me. Like that would happen, but it was sort of weird.

We passed through the oversized florals and out into the hot air. At least there was a cover over the main door where people parked to check-in. No cars waited right at the moment and Natalie didn't employ valet service. It's not like she needed to. The parking lot was huge.

We kept walking until we were on the verge between the parking lot and the street.

"I didn't want to talk inside," Natalie said. "The witch

council has a couple of people here. They even brought someone in like they were going to watch her!"

"That was Flori, the woman who tried to get into my café super early this morning. Or at least her spirit did," I said.

"I heard," Natalie said, keeping her voice low and looking back. "But you never know what else they're looking into."

"I wanted to talk to them," I said.

Natalie looked at me like I'd just said I wanted to go wrestle a dragon or something.

"I want to know where Flori got her magic. She's so powerful that it's odd that she doesn't seem to know she's a witch. That means her folks don't know or understand and that's really unusual."

"Adopted?" Natalie suggested.

"She'd have been adopted by witches with her power." Witches tended to keep track of each other. It was all part of staying under the radar and not being noticed by non-magical people. There were far more normal folks than there were witches. We might have more power individually, but non-magicals could make life hell for us, which we'd learned through history. Now, we just pretended to be ordinary, at least as much as we could.

Babies don't have any control so if a witch couple had a baby with power and they died early on, the witch council would make sure the child was adopted into a witch family.

It wasn't unheard of for two non-magical people to have a baby with power. Somewhere back in the ancestry, someone probably had power and the child inherited the magic. It would be highly unusual for a child with Flori's level of power to appear in a non-magical family, though. It was hard to believe that she'd never just done something without any control before this. I had an even harder time believing that no other unscrupulous witch had tried to take advantage of her.

Natalie cocked her head and raised her hand to her chin. "That is interesting. Especially when you consider the timing."

"She did run into Mrs. Ainsley," I said.

"That's right. Do you think Mrs. Ainsley stole the book and murdered Eric? That nasty part of her is wicked enough," Natalie said.

"I don't know about murdering someone. I mean, he was hit, hard. And she's old. No matter how weird she gets when she talks, she still doesn't seem to have much body strength. And from my understanding, the murder left quite a mess."

"But you think she might be involved with Flori?"

"Maybe?" Now I was confused. Flori had magic when she ran into Mrs. Ainsley. A lot. And they hadn't spent time together. You'd think that Flori would recognize the woman if Mrs. Ainsley had put a spell on her. I mean there are concealing spells, but Flori's power was pretty major. Even untrained she would have suspected something. I could be wrong having always had magic and always having an understanding of what I could and couldn't do.

"If she was adopted or something, maybe Mrs. Ainsley used her as a crime of opportunity?" I suggested. My ideas were falling apart and I hadn't even talked to the witch council.

"Let's go in and see the council witches. They're WBI so they're more used to dealing with ordinary witches. Maybe they'll be nice and tell us a little something about Flori. You did call them," Natalie said. I could tell she didn't believe that they'd be helpful for a second.

I had to admit I was pretty sure I didn't believe that either.

Naturally, Natalie knew exactly where the witches were staying. Top floor, of course. Council witches, even those that just work for the WBI, always got the best and the view up there was the best there was. I mean it wasn't like the view was going to send anyone into throes of ecstasy, but it was quite nice. And worthwhile.

Whenever I followed Natalie through the hotel I always caught faint traces of what I thought of as new-car smell. When I was younger I'd talked to her about it, trying to figure out where it came from and what was used to get that smell, but she'd never understood what I was talking about. The smell was so familiar to her that it was just a normal aroma.

The hallways upstairs had no music but I heard a television from one of the rooms we passed. It wasn't loud, but I didn't know if that was a tribute to the soundproofing, probably magical, in the walls or if the person inside had the television sound on low.

People in hotels always interested me. I wanted to know what had brought them to the place, how the room compared to other hotels they'd stayed in, whether they were happy to be in the city they were staying in, or if they wanted to be elsewhere. A part of me envied Natalie and her ability to get the answers to some of those questions just by being friendly at the front desk. Another part of me was thankful I didn't have to ask those questions for fear that I might not like the answers.

Natalie knocked on the door. We waited for what seemed like far too long. I could have answered the door in a far larger home before I heard anyone even move inside. I fidgeted next to Natalie.

She put a hand on mine.

A moment later, I felt the traces of a spell. They were assessing who we were before opening the door. Maybe for our protection or maybe for their own, with a guess that the latter was far more important.

"What?" Blondie opened the door only far enough to peek out at us. She didn't look any happier than she had early this morning, though if I had had to be up for as long as she was, I might be a bit on the cranky side, too. In fact, the crankiness was probably what led me right to her door.

"Where did Flori get her magic?" I asked.

Blondie frowned and drew back. The door was still open only a crack but her hold had loosened as if my question had come out of left field. Finally, she recovered herself and looked back out.

"Why?"

"The book in the special library's archives was supposed to be on how to make an ordinary pet into a familiar. I would guess that it had something to do with finding a way to let an ordinary creature have magic. Could someone have used that spell on a human? Like Flori?" I asked. It was an odd question but it would explain her power.

Blondie leaned back and opened the door a bit wider. She

stepped back. "Not the kind of conversation to have in the hallway."

Natalie and I went in, though I noticed Natalie hung back long enough to let me go first. That was unusual. Natalie always goes first, wanting to lead.

The room was a pretty ordinary hotel room. A hallway going in, the bathroom door on the right. The main area included two queen-sized beds on the right and a low dresser with a television on it and a desk on the left. Two chairs and a small round table were in the left corner.

Red was in one of the chairs. Flori was on the bed closest to the wall, apparently asleep, though I saw the bonds of magic that held her down. Dampening magic. Ties to keep her there. And something I didn't quite recognize. It felt wrong to go sniffing around too closely at the spells the WBI witches had put down.

"You are?" Red asked.

"I'm Jade. This is Natalie."

Red nodded. "The hotelier. And the familiar café owner."

I nodded.

"Call me Red." Like I hadn't been thinking of her that way already. Not exactly original on her part. "And that's Blade."

I wanted to repeat the name but bit my tongue. It wasn't politic to go around acting as if you thought someone's name, even a nickname or a false name for the purposes of work, was strange. I glanced at Natalie. She didn't appear surprised by the names, which meant the witches had used those when checking in. Their credentials, magicked as they were, would have had those names on them as well.

"She wants to know where Flori got her magic," Blade said, her voice quieter, softer in tone than it had been at the door. "Like maybe it was connected to that missing book."

Red looked thoughtful. "Like someone wanted to know if they could make someone else magical."

I nodded.

"My understanding is that the person giving the non-familiar magic would have to give up some of their own. Magic isn't just created out of nothing."

Magic took an ability to sense and understand the subtle energies. It wasn't like making a blind person see, where you just manipulated cells that were already there. You had to create something from nothing. It would require that you offer something to create it. The best offerings were those that were close to what was needed.

If a blind person had no eyes, well then, offering eyes would be good, though the eyes could be symbolic. A practitioner with enough power, will, and belief could probably use the eye of a potato and make the magic work. A lesser practitioner could make do with the eye of an animal or even a dead human, though the eye of a living human would always be optimal.

"Could they have taken someone else's magical powers?" I asked. Eric had magic. He was pretty powerful, though not at Flori's level.

"You're thinking the librarian who was murdered?" Red asked.

Blade was nodding. "Taking someone's magic would probably kill them. Perhaps beating them was done to keep anyone from looking too closely at their magic. It looked like an ordinary murder."

Red turned her head to look at me. "But why are they after you and your familiars?"

"Maybe they need more magic and want to try a familiar?" I said, considering. I knew the background of all the cats in the café. They really were familiars, had been bred with magic. None had any mysterious beginning.

"Maybe..." Red didn't seem convinced. "You could be a

distraction. Or perhaps they're looking more closely at you directly. You are not without a fair bit of power…"

And, I thought, it would make Trinity look doubly guilty if I were killed, especially if anyone noticed I'd lost my power before dying. Trinity and I were often together. It would put her in prison, though she was innocent. The question of why Trinity suggested that there was more thought put into this than before.

"Did Sarah Meyerson have any books on transferring magic?" I asked. "Seeing her shop was burning when I came over this way."

Red and Blade looked at each other. "Not to our knowledge, but sometimes things slip through the council. We're going to need more investigators here."

Red looked at Natalie. "I suggest you make sure you have one or two more rooms available for this evening."

Natalie sighed, glanced at me, and then left to go see what she could do to find a room for more WBI witches. Suddenly I was even happier than I didn't work at her hotel. I wouldn't want to have to face the person I had just had to cancel a room for.

Natalie could do it, though. Of that, I had no doubt.

I turned back to Blade and Red, not sure what they wanted with me.

B lade tapped a hand on the desk, her eyes unfocused. On an ordinary human, I would have thought she was thinking. I knew better. Blade was a witch, probably quite powerful. She was doing a spell. I felt the waves of it wash over me seconds later. Cool magic, cleansing. Searching, too.

"You've got reserves you've never used," Blade said.

I shrugged. I knew I had a fair amount of power. It was always enough for whatever I needed to do, but I rarely found the need to push my boundaries. I worked with the public, always had, even at the shelter, which meant I understood the need to hide my powers. No reason to get lazy about things. Some witches loved pushing their limits. Several worked at the college here, where they could work in a witch-only setting and testing spells and their power, see what their limits were, test new theories.

"Flori's spirit could have gone to the café because magic recognized magic," Red said. "It may not have targeted Jade specifically. More like the café, with its protections, felt safe. Whoever put the magic in her might have been trying to move the magic into someone else, someone they were closer to."

"Fiona and Isaac," I said. "I heard Isaac didn't have much magic, or maybe none at all, depending upon who you talked to. Could Fiona be doing it? She wouldn't want to use Isaac first. She clearly loves him."

Her love might have been a bit too much, or a bit too lenient, but it was clear she cared. I shuddered at the thought of that child with the amount of magic that Flori had.

"According to the library, Eric said the book went missing the night before. He'd discovered it that evening and yelled at Trinity in the morning. Fiona and Isaac didn't get into town before the special library closed the day before. We checked them out thoroughly because Isaac was a witness," Blade said.

"You said you saw an older woman with them but you didn't recognize her? We had reports of the older woman as well, though we haven't seen her," Red said.

"Yes. Someone was with Fiona like they were trying to soothe her when she was crying on the steps of the library after they found Eric." I tried to picture the older woman, the one I thought was Fiona's mother. Once again, it was hard to remember her. "And she was there when Natalie and I were at dinner."

"Didn't Natalie say they had all checked in together?" I asked, thinking that I had asked Natalie about them and she had said all three. Maybe not.

"No. Only Fiona and Isaac were staying here, according to Natalie, though she did mention another person with them," Red said. She stood up and glanced at Blade. "I'll go."

"We shouldn't go without backup," Blade argued.

"Someone has to watch the girl," Red argued.

Blade glanced at me. I wasn't sure what they wanted from me. Did I need to watch Flori? If someone came for her, I couldn't protect her more than she was. I could protect myself but I didn't have offensive spells. It had never inter-ested me. Did they want me to go track down the elderly woman I'd seen with Fiona? Ask Natalie about her?

"She can't," Red said. "No training."

Blade sighed. "I'll stay. You go. But don't hesitate to call for help. Flori is well tied down."

Not only was Flori magically tied down, she was at the top of a hotel which would slow her down. She didn't know spells. I suddenly wondered if the spell was so intricate I hadn't been able to get a handle on what it did was a protec-tion spell against someone trying to take her spirit. Given that such negative magic would be noticed by the council, I wondered if the two witches had a backup plan. One that could put Blade or Red in danger.

"What if it's a setup?" I asked. "To split you up?"

Red glanced at me. "You think someone would try to take my magic?"

"If there are enough witches, even the most powerful can be taken down," I said. History told us that. Even ordinary folks could take down a powerful witch.

"I'll have to hope that your town has a strong enough police department and that Blade will get there fast enough." Red turned and left without another word.

I left shortly after Red. Blade made it clear she had no use for me in the room. When I reached the lobby, I noticed Natalie busy at the front desk. I gave a small wave, not wanting to interrupt, and hurried out of the building. I texted her a quick note after I got to my car. I got a thumbs-up back, which meant she was too busy to reply though she clearly wanted to talk.

The café wasn't terribly busy when I returned. I noted a large group of witches in the familiar room, the most we could accommodate at one time. Good. I charged people to enter the familiar room on a per-person basis. I tried to limit the room to a single group, though I wasn't always able to do that. I knew I was leaving money on the table, as they say, but it felt more appropriate to do so.

This group was definitely a moneymaker. I noticed a couple of frappuccino cups sitting on the tables.

"Did you hear anything more about Sarah Meyerson's?" I asked. Jason was behind the counter. Charlene had a cleaning rag in her hand. I slipped behind the serving area intending to grab an apron

"Sarah's alive," Charlene said. "She'd been in the bookstore when the fire started but was in the back. I guess the fire department found her. Someone used magic to make sure she'd live until the paramedics got there and she could be taken to the hospital. Bongo had been spelled to sleep, too. He's going to live, but I guess he was much more iffy," Charlene said, keeping her voice down. "Her employee grabbed Shayla, fortunately."

Charlene could speak freely as no customers hovered around the cafe. That wasn't unusual for Saturday afternoon. As the child of a WBI officer, Charlene would have noticed anyone listening in that shouldn't hear what she had to say.

"But they'll all be okay?" I asked.

"I think they already are," Charlene said. She wanted to be clear that she didn't have inside knowledge.

"Do they know anything about what started the fire?" I leaned a bit on the counter. While I was mentally ready to go, to search out any clue to who had been hurting people in town, my body was saying I needed to rest.

"They think it was a spell," Jason said, his voice low, almost in awe.

That was bad. Whoever did it would be charged not only with arson but they'd face the council. While you couldn't take magic from someone without harm, you could dampen their magic and keep them from accessing it. It wasn't an uncommon punishment for those who used their magic illegally or indiscriminately. Starting a fire was certainly both.

"No one else in the bookstore was hurt?" I asked.

Both shook their heads. "The girl working got customers out right away before grabbing Shayla. I'm not sure she even knew Sarah was back there," Jason said.

The bell rang and Joyce hurried in to start work. She waved at Charlene who pulled the rag from her shoulder. It was about time for Charlene to head home. I smiled, though my mind was still on the fire.

Sarah could have been talking to whoever started the fire. Or maybe the arsonist just wanted to cause trouble, to focus attention elsewhere. A fire would definitely do it. Tons of folks had been out on the street looking at the fire, though, so far as I knew, all the open shops had been attended.

Other places would be less attended and perhaps not even noticed. I thought about the Lyons office next door. They'd have the most information about Trinity's case there, more even than the police because Tyson would have been searching for ways to keep Trinity out of jail.

I pulled out my phone and called him again. I wasn't even thinking. Just doing it. When Tyson answered, again, I realized this was the second time in a day I'd called him about something that was probably stupid. My face got hot. I hoped he didn't think I was just calling to try and find a reason to talk to him.

"What if the fire was a distraction?" I said, without a greeting. "What if someone wanted the notes you might have on Trinity's case in the office?"

"Seems like a lot to go through," Tyson said.

"But with all the smoke and people around, someone could work on getting in," I said.

"Protection spells," Tyson reminded me.

"The fire was next door. Mine would warn me about it. Did yours?"

Tyson was silent. "No." Dread filled his voice. "I've got to go."

He hung up.

I put my phone away and hurried out the front door. So much for me helping at the café. I was definitely going to have to make it up to my workers. They'd been troopers through all of this.

The fire department had finished their work. The engines were gone but inspectors were still at the site, making notes. The front of the building was still standing, though the glass had broken. Yellow tape warned me away from that part of the sidewalk. I stepped out into the street to walk around. The building smelled burnt and wet. I couldn't imagine what Sarah was going through, knowing what had happened to her shop on top of the worry about Bongo at the vet without her.

It didn't take me another minute to get to Tyson's. I peered into the window, putting my hands around my face to try and make out more details. Nothing looked out of place, not in the front, but then it wouldn't. Tyson wouldn't keep anything important out in the reception area. He'd keep it back in his office or something. Maybe the office had a designated room for cases in progress. I supposed it would depend upon how large the files were.

I reached out for the door to try the knob. I expected it to be locked, to keep me out. Instead, the door opened easily, swinging inside, on silent hinges. The bell over the door sounded, too loud and hollow in the empty building. I paused in the doorway.

"Tyson?" I called.

I heard nothing. He couldn't have beaten me to the office. He didn't live that close. I stepped over the threshold into the reception area. I chanted a small spell under my breath, enhancing my senses. I felt the area rug under my feet giving way beneath my weight. I heard the ticking of a clock in a room down the hall, the faintest tick tick that I'd never have noted if not for the enhancement.

Smoke from outside reached my nose, almost overwhelming me with the stink of it. I coughed, the sound too loud in the near silent office. Outside, a car passed by making me jump just a bit.

I felt magic in the air. Someone had done a spell. It pressed against my temples, made me want to turn and run. The last might have been a remnant of the protection spell Tyson had on the office, but I couldn't be certain. My head began to throb, just a little. I focused on the trail of the spell. The sensation came from in front of me, deeper in the building. Either the protection spell had been done in the offices themselves, not impossible as that's where the most important files would be, or this wasn't a protection spell.

I breathed shallowly, not wanting to get another strong whiff of the smoke, and made my way to the door that would take me back to the offices. I should have turned around and left. It wasn't legal for me to be there, but I knew something was wrong. Very wrong.

I pushed the door open. The hairs on my arms rose. I no longer felt alone. I felt watched. I tried to determine what made me feel that way but I noticed only the cream-colored walls glaring at me. I glanced up, wondering if there were cameras, but my eyes found nothing, though I did see the faintest imperfection in the paint on the ceiling.

"Tyson?" I called, though I knew he couldn't be there.

Nothing.

I felt chilled. I backed out of the office heading towards the front door. I half-expected to feel a hand grab me from behind, pulling me back inside. Instead, I made it outside without incident. As I got to the door and turned back, the very lack of an attack was almost as scary as if someone had tried to grab me. I paused in the doorway and used my phone to call Tyson again.

At least he answered.

"I went down to your office. The door was unlocked," I said. "No one was in the front."

"Stay out," Tyson said. "The door should have been locked up. I'm almost there."

I waited by the door, looking in. At least if someone were inside, I'd see them if they tried to leave through the front. Not that anyone would be that foolish. Too bad I hadn't brought someone with me who could watch the back.

I paced around the front. I watched Tyson's car drive past, going far too fast for the road, particularly with the police tape in front of Sarah's building. He rounded the corner and parked there. It was probably closer than any other spot. During the week he wouldn't have found a spot on the street so close.

I watched as he jumped out of the car, his khaki shorts falling to mid-thigh. He had on sneakers and socks that fell down around his ankles. His pullover shirt was neatly done, at least. Tyson normally takes much better care of his appearance. The socks were a clear indication that he'd rushed out of the house.

He slowed as he got near me. He placed a hand on the doorframe and closed his eyes. He would be trying to get a read on the protection spell and how it was breached. He nodded.

"Someone used powerful negative magic to get past the spell," he said. "Can you smell it?"

Some witches could smell magic. I wasn't one of them. Until then, I hadn't realized that Tyson was.

I shook my head. "I don't smell magic."

"It just smells so strong to me. Can you feel anything?" he asked.

"I felt magic when I went in. Like someone was wrapping a band around my head," I said. That sensation could have been any number of things.

Tyson frowned. He stepped through the door. I followed, alert to any sensation of negative magic. The office felt colder than usual, but it could have been me. I'd been standing out in the hot sun for several minutes.

My fingers tingled with a chill, different from the chill of Flori's spirit when she'd been in the café. Tyson's shoes squeaked as he crossed the wood floor to the hall door.

I followed so close behind him that I not only smelled the spicy scent of the soap he used but felt the heat from his body. I rubbed my arms, looking around his back, hoping to see something I'd missed earlier.

Tyson pushed the hallway door open. Once again, the space felt too quiet, waiting.

He glanced back at me, started to speak, and then stopped. He turned and looked back into the hallway, hesitating before walking down it.

I wondered if he smelled negative magic. I certainly felt something, though I couldn't have pinpointed what it was. The hallway just felt too quiet and filled with a stillness that felt like waiting.

Tyson took a careful step into the hall. Paused. Another step. Pause.

I nearly ran into him as I stepped into the hall behind him, letting the door close. He was so close I could have wrapped my arms around him.

The door on the right was the closest. Tyson took another step and opened it. The tiniest of squeaks from the latch sounded overly loud in the silence. After peering in, he left the door open while he continued to the door on the left, still walking slowly and quietly, alert for anything in the silence.

The knob on this one made a click when turned. The hairs on my neck raised. The door didn't squeak as it opened. I caught the faintest scent of dampness from the room but it was gone as quickly as it had come. Tyson looked in. He shook his head backing out.

There were four more doors along the hallway. One no doubt led to a conference room, which I'd heard about.

Another probably led to a bathroom. The door on the end was the exterior door as denoted by the exit sign glowing green above it. The final one was probably a store room or something.

The conference room was on the right, notable by the glass door and walls, covered with blinds. Tyson reached that door with me practically stepping on his shoes. He pushed open that door, which was not latched.

He drew in a breath, a quiet gasp of air before stepping inside.

I moved closer, looking around him to see blood on the floor. Dark hair poked out from beyond the table.

I didn't recognize the hair. I backed out to make a call to the police. While I could have called 911—it was certainly possible this wasn't magic related—too much had gone on to suggest that it wasn't. I needed experts in magic and I needed them now. Someone had clearly broken in through a protection spell using very strong, very negative magic.

My voice sounded too loud in the hallway when I reported a break-in at the Lyons Law Offices.

I'd barely finished when someone reached up behind me and snatched my phone. I whirled around in time to see a woman with short blue-black hair regarding me, her skin peachy-pale and her eyes brown pits that I almost believed held a hint of sadness, even as the hand not holding my phone grabbed my wrist and began to twist, hard.

Tyson turned from where he knelt by the blood on the floor to see me struggling with the woman. He stood quickly, hurrying over, only to be stopped by an invisible wall. Perhaps a trap from earlier. Perhaps the dark-haired woman was just that good.

"What do you want?" I screamed at her.

The woman just smiled. I felt magic around me, thick, heavy, foggy magic that threatened to move up into my nose and mouth to keep me from breathing.

I chanted a quick spell of my own, enough to give me a bit of breathing room, though it wasn't going to hold long. I hoped it would keep her spell at bay until help arrived. I mentally sent another scream for magical help, flooding the call with what I knew.

The last time I'd had to call for help, I'd felt the thought floating away. This thought started to leave but was stuffed back into my head. Pain lanced through my skull and down my back as if my skull had been pounded by a rock. Another spell from this woman.

"Who are you?" I asked. Tyson was still trying to break

through the invisible wall. I saw him open his mouth to call out but heard nothing. So not just keeping him out but isolating both of us.

"Don't you recognize me?" she asked.

"No," I said. I searched her face for some clue. While I had hints of having seen her before, I couldn't place her.

I didn't know anyone with eyes as dark as hers. The shape of her lips offered a hint to me as if I'd seen someone with lips like that before, but it wasn't someone I knew well. I tried to picture everyone I knew, fitting them to her mouth but no one was close.

She leaned her face close to me, whispering something, though her mouth was open wide as if she were yelling. I felt my shields start to fall, her magic not just floating in through my nose and mouth but pulling at me, like a thousand tiny hands, attempting to rip me apart.

The dark-haired woman was trying to steal my magic! The terror of dying right there right then pushed me to fight harder, though I would have said I was doing all I could before.

I reached down deep. I knew Mason wasn't far from me, just a few doors down. This witch might not know that. Certainly, she wouldn't know about his connection to the other familiars.

I thrust my will out towards him, letting him know what I needed, hoping it would get through where the call wouldn't. The call was general, public. Calling for Mason was much more personal and her spell wouldn't necessarily block that.

A rush of magic came back just an instant later, though I felt as if I were hanging half out of my body.

The sudden infusion of magic, of protection magic, threw the witch off of me. The spell pressing against me, drawing my magic, wavered.

I pulled my spirit back into my body, feeling the mental

snap as things went back in place. My own magic felt worn and tired, but I put up another shield around myself, one as strong as the one she'd put up around Tyson.

I felt Mason float off, worried, but so fatigued he couldn't remain with me any longer. I needed to get to him.

The witch turned towards Tyson, tearing down the wall she'd made. She hurled herself at him. She grabbed him by the shoulders and leaned in closer to him, her mouth open like she was going to bite. Only then did I remember that she'd done the same to me.

I felt magic coming from Tyson. I thought I saw his spirit fighting to stay in his body. His familiar wasn't close enough to help.

I ran through all the spells I knew. Nothing.

Instead, all I had was a schoolgirl's spell to throw papers around. Using what I had, I sent all the paper in the conference room flying towards her. My augmented powers pulled paper from the cabinets at the far end of the room and those spun towards the woman, flying at her like hundreds of paper birds.

Her hand went up to protect herself. That was enough to allow Tyson to draw his spirit back inside his body and push her away.

She fell backward, towards me. I stepped back, not wanting to catch her. Tyson moved forward quickly, probably hoping to keep her off balance.

I let the papers fall where they were. I worried about the person on the floor, injured and bleeding, or perhaps dead. I hoped the papers wouldn't hurt them further.

Just then someone grabbed my shoulder and pulled me back. I turned to face this new threat, but it was only Officer Tom Alsez and the WBI witch, Red.

Behind them were more officers. Red had a hand up, her eyes half-closed.

Tyson stood, hands ready with another spell, waiting.

"Tyson," I said. "It's okay."

He looked up at me, puzzled. Then he dropped his hands, stepping back from the witch woman. He turned behind him and went back to the woman on the floor. It hit me then that it was probably Deborah. My stomach sank as I sent out a thread of magic to detect anyone else alive in the room.

It wasn't until the next day that I understood what had happened. My mom had come to stay with me, which I felt bad about. It's not like my little apartment has any good guest space so she'd slept on the sofa. Mason had cuddled with me. Joyce and Jason had made sure the familiar cats were all taken care of. None had any undue issues after Mason had drawn their magic to me for use.

Mason, though, was knocked out, pretty much like me. Mom fed us both quite well. Mason got plenty of treats along with his canned food favorites. He even got extra cups of the crunchy food that he liked. I got spaghetti, plenty of garlic bread, and all the soda I could drink. The sugar helped keep me grounded, which I needed.

Natalie came over first thing the next morning to check on me.

While I'd been sleeping and trying to help the police when I could, Natalie had been absorbing the gossip that was swirling around town. She left the problems of scheduling rooms to her front desk people, but it ended up working out that the rooms she needed were available. Things like that happen for Natalie.

We talked over breakfast, my mom reassuring me that she'd arranged for my shift to be covered and that someone would take care of the familiars downstairs.

Natalie told me what she'd learned the day before, though more information was still forthcoming.

"The witch that attacked you was Joyce Williamson," Natalie said quietly, waiting for my reaction.

"Wasn't that the old woman with Fiona? Her mother?" I asked between bites of food. My mother watched as I ate, ready to add something if I appeared to need more fuel. Doing heavy magic gives one an appetite.

"Not her mother, but her aunt," Natalie said. She sipped some orange juice my mother must have brought with her. "She lives in Knoxville." Knoxville Tennessee was just about a little over a half day's drive from Waverton.

"That child of Fiona's," my mother said, "didn't have much magic and apparently that's an issue for Fiona. He'd be worn out doing the smallest spell or even a ritual. Instead of making sure he didn't do too much, Fiona was very critical."

Natalie added that Isaac's father and Fiona were both really powerful.I guess that was an issue for Fiona.

"I talked to Trinity and she heard from Lani that Joyce was visiting specialty libraries looking to help Isaac," Natalie said.

My mother rolled her eyes. Really, nothing short of pretty negative magic would have helped Isaac.

"She finally ended up in Waverton. I guess Isaac had reached out to Trinity about a project he was doing—you know for one of the kiddie witch enrichment classes—and Trinity had responded. He mentioned the project and Joyce figured that Waverton wasn't all that far so she'd check it out.

Joyce figured she'd been everywhere else and decided to

check into the familiar library. She'd checked into the hotel about two weeks ago and that was when she found the book about making non-magical creatures magical. She'd taken careful notes.

She'd tried it on a homeless boy in Nashville, drawing the magic from an elderly male witch under hospice care. Nothing had happened. At first, Joyce was certain it was because the older man was dying, but as she looked over her notes, she wondered if she hadn't missed something.

"It's what happens when you start down a negative path. You always second guess yourself," my mother inserted, giving me a long look, as if I were about to jump into trying negative spells.

Joyce came back to Waverton and read some more, not just the spell, but the information about the spell. She'd wanted to read longer, but her eyesight was failing her and she was having a difficult time focusing.

"And that's where it gets really nasty," Natalie said. She paused for dramatic effect. "Joyce was so annoyed that she couldn't keep reading she started thinking about ways she could adapt that spell, like to help keep her from aging!"

Back in Nashville, Joyce hunted down a wild rabbit that had some magic and used the spell on herself. Her magic increased only slightly as the rabbit hadn't been a very powerful familiar, but her joints started to feel better.

It was then that she'd called Fiona and suggested she needed to be in Waverton. Joyce had originally thought that she'd take the lives of several familiars. Her first instinct was the café because the cats would be accessible to the public.

"But I don't let people in with the familiars without an appointment," I protested.

Natalie held up a hand.

"She learned that," my mom said before Natalie could respond. "And I heard that that's why she dropped the idea of the café because you'd notice who'd been there when all the familiars were dead. But that didn't stop her. She was hoping to use other familiars. It's why they visited so many places. Getting the lay of the land!" My mom said that last almost proudly. While she had to have heard the expression before, I had a feeling she'd waited to use it in conversation long before this.

"Naturally," Natalie jumped back in before my mother could continue, "Fiona didn't want to use Isaac as a guinea pig."

"Can you imagine?" my mother said.

"Fiona figured Joyce was a powerful witch and getting older so maybe she was imaging things," Natalie said.

"I heard that Fiona thought she might be getting a bit senile," Mom added.

"But she still agreed to come to Waverton with Isaac. To make sure they had an excuse, Joyce insisted that Fiona call one of the vets about her bird to give her a reason to be in town." Natalie picked at one of the muffins that still sat on the table. My mom had gotten a dozen for the three of us.

"She really did think this through." Mom glared at Natalie in case I wanted more muffins.

"Fiona confessed to all of this," Natalie added. "Her bird wasn't sick at all, either. Just her aunt, I guess. If doing a bunch of negative magic is a sickness."

Some people thought it was.

I kept on shoveling eggs into my mouth. Fortunately, my mom had made plenty for me. She and Natalie had finished theirs long ago.

Natalie continued telling me what happened.

Joyce arrived the day before, though she'd stayed out of town. She knew Fiona would let her stay with her and she wanted no ties to the town for herself, particularly since she'd decided to steal the book, which she did that afternoon.

Fiona and Isaac arrived that evening. Joyce had stayed in their room, just like she'd planned. First thing in the morning, Fiona went to the library intending to do some reading of her own, not realizing that Joyce had stolen the book. Stealing a book with as much information on negative magic as that one contained was a major enough offense that Joyce hadn't trusted her niece with the information about what she'd done. Instead, she let her go to the library.

While Eric had noticed something odd about the archives the day before and noted the missing book, he'd not worried about it too much, just reporting it in the morning. Getting a request for it first thing had set him off, which started the altercation with Trinity. That worked in Joyce's favor, though she knew that she'd be found out if Eric kept looking.

So she'd made sure the written information was misplaced. Then, she'd hit Eric over the head. He hadn't died. It gave her an idea. She wanted to show Fiona the spells worked. Flori had wandered into the special library. Her friends had decided to stay outside, thinking it was too nice to go in.

"That poor girl," Mom said. "I do hope she's getting the help she needs. Imagine not even knowing you're a witch and then having all this magic inserted into you. I can't say that I approve of the way she acted—Natalie explained it— but still. Such a shock to a young girl."

"So she had some magic?" I asked.

"Just enough to keep her from being susceptible to our do not enter spells. I heard she liked the cooler air and she'd talked a little to Trinity," Natalie said.

When no one was around, Joyce had used Flori to demonstrate the spell, imbuing the girl with Eric's not unsubstantial amount of magic. He'd died quietly, but not before blood had begun to leak from his nose, eyes, and ears, which was why everyone talked about the murder being so horrible.

"I heard she even used a chair to beat him to make sure it looked like he'd been bludgeoned instead of having his magic stolen," Mom said. She shuddered.

After my experience with the feeling of pressure and the pulling of magic from my body, I felt sorry for him. He must have suffered. I might not have liked Eric, even thought he was a rather nasty person, but I didn't think anyone should have had to go through what he did.

"Fiona says she was horrified to find out what Joyce was doing. She ran outside. Isaac stayed," Natalie said. She made a face like what could you expect from that horrible child.

"The poor boy was getting so much pressure from his mother about using magic that it's no wonder he stayed," Mom said more kindly. "I mean who wouldn't be intrigued by a way to get something you've always been told you need to have?"

I nodded. I could understand.

"Why say Trinity did it?" I asked.

"She'd talked to Flori earlier and she'd corresponded with Isaac. Joyce didn't want anyone to notice that Flori hadn't had much magic nor did she want to take the chance that Trinity remembered a school kid named Isaac. Plus, Eric had yelled at Trinity about the missing book. It seemed perfect. Joyce just didn't realize that Trinity would have a standing morning break date with two of her best friends, keeping her out of the library at the critical time." Natalie gave a nod to make her point.

"It didn't stop her from being arrested," I said. "And held in jail."

"Tyson actually made sure she stayed there," Natalie said. "The first day after her arrest and questioning, Deborah suggested that whoever did this would be easier to catch if they thought everyone was looking at Trinity. The police went along with it. Tyson reported it to the council as well, so there were no black marks against her."

"He never told us!" I said.

"And I let him know what I thought of that," Natalie said. "We could have been killed. But he was worried that the more people who knew, the more likely that word would get out. Mrs. DiAngelo did try to warn us away."

I fumed at that. As if I couldn't be trusted to keep my mouth shut. Tyson was going to get a piece of my mind.

Natalie continued to tell me the story.

"Joyce liked that she could move easier after the rabbit and she wanted more power. She didn't really like killing people, so she started experimenting. Poor Mrs. Ainsley and her companions got the whammy and that's part of the reason Mrs. Ainsley was so freaky," Natalie said.

"Those two women with your Mrs. Ainsley just got kind of thick but Mrs. Ainsley was already slipping into dementia and she started acting like she had multiple personalities or something." Natalie looked at my mom before glancing back at a muffin. I was still hungry but wouldn't begrudge my friend something. It's not like my stomach had no limits.

"I almost feel bad for Mrs. Ainsley," I said. "How horrible. Now that she's not having someone draw her powers, will she get back to normal?" She had been a rather sweet-tempered older lady even if she did dabble on the dark side.

Natalie shrugged. No one knew. The doctors actually had more hope for her companions than for Mrs. Ainsley given that they were just foggy. Mrs. Ainsley's pre-existing dementia was less likely to be reversed.

"That poor young Flori had all these powers but didn't know what to do about it. She came back here on her own hoping to figure it out. I heard that Flori got some of Eric's knowledge as well as his power but she didn't understand why she knew things." Mom got up and went to the kitchen to make another pot of coffee.

"Joyce noticed her. I mean she gave Flori her powers so she had a sense of where she was, if that makes sense," Natalie said.

It didn't, not really, but it wasn't like I was an expert on negative magic.

"So Joyce figured an ordinary girl like Flori wouldn't be missed. She probably even planned to dump her body somewhere outside of town." Natalie looked hopefully at my mom who was making more coffee. "But apparently, while Flori might not have understood exactly what was going on, Eric's knowledge and her power allowed her to fight off Joyce. She sent her spirit to the only place she could think of that felt safe. Your café."

"So that's why the protection spell didn't keep her out. She was looking for protection herself, not trying to harm my familiars," I said.

Natalie nodded and continued.

When she realized the council had sent the WBI and were possibly looking for her, Joyce fled. She'd hoped to find someone with enough magic that she could dodge the WBI witches. Deborah was the unfortunate witch deemed the most powerful.

Joyce had entered Tyson's office with Deborah, pretending to be someone who had questions about Trinity's case. Deborah hadn't spent enough time in Waverton to know that Joyce wasn't a relative and she'd let her in. Hence the protection spells weren't set off, though the door hadn't been locked. Deborah hadn't planned on staying long.

The fire in Sarah's building was supposed to consume the attorney's office as well, but Joyce, having never worked in a small witch business didn't know that even the weakest witch business owner with the tiniest shop knows to spell their building against fire and theft. She'd been lucky to get the fire at Sarah's to burn as much as it had.

"You'd think with all the planning she had started with, she'd have thought to look into those things." My mom clicked her tongue as she poured more coffee for Natalie and me.

And then Tyson and I had come around. She knew I was waiting outside. Joyce had gotten greedy and was hoping to get more magic and perhaps more youth. Tyson and I may not have felt as powerful, but we had magic, and she still wasn't at the level of health and age that she wanted to be.

"But you fought her off!" Natalie clapped her hands together as if I'd won a prize.

"Not alone," I said. "I was lucky Mason was there and that he had the bond he has with the other familiars."

Mom and Natalie watched while I stuffed as much food as I could into my mouth. I was still starving. Mason and I had been doing an awful lot of big magic lately. I glanced down at Mason and noted his dish was empty but he was stretched out by my feet resting comfortably, clearly listening to our conversation.

"Where's Trinity?" I asked.

"Tyson is still in the hospital. He was hurt more than you were," Mom said. "She said she'll be by later."

"I ought to go visit, too," I said. I mean, it was Tyson.

"We'll go tomorrow. There won't be so many family members there."

It was probably good. Then I wouldn't be trying to steal the food from Tyson's plate while I talked to him. Of course, at least then he wouldn't think I was still crushing on him after all this time. Not that I was. Not really.

I got a text on my phone and turned it over to look at who it was from. The way my heart flipped over and my stomach started dancing when I saw Tyson's name may have given a lie to my lack of a crush.

But he was worried about me. After what happened to him.

He thought that I'd saved his life. He wanted to take me to dinner—not right away of course because no one could afford to feed us just then—but maybe next weekend.

I put my phone away and tried to hide my smiles by shoveling more food in my mouth. It might have fooled my mom, but Natalie was giving me a look. She knew something was up and I had no doubt that as soon as Mom left, she was going to give me the third degree.

And that bothered me because as a team, we'd proven we were pretty good detectives. She was sure to find out that I was excited about dinner alone with Tyson.

Heck, given what Natalie and I had found out, we could freelance as investigators, for witches. Of course, that might cut into my time with Tyson, assuming our celebratory dinner wasn't our only outing. Maybe the cat café would be enough.

Mason sneezed and then got up and meowed, wanting more food. Or maybe he agreed that I ought to stick to focusing on the café. Probably both.

ABOUT BONNIE ELIZABETH

Bonnie Elizabeth could never decide what to do, so she wrote stories about amazing things and sometimes she even finished them.

While rejection stung her so badly in person, she spent most of her young life talking to cats and dogs rather than people, she was unusually resilient when it came to rejections on her writing, racking up a good number of them.

Floating through a variety of jobs, including veterinary receptionist, cemetery administrator, and finally acupuncturist, she continued to write stories.

When the internet came along (yes she's old), she started blogging as her cat, because we all know cats don't notice rejection. Then she started publishing.

Bonnie writes in a variety of genres. Her popular Whisper series is contemporary fantasy and her Teenage Fairy Godmother series is written for teens. She has been published in a number of anthologies and is working on expanding her writing repertoire.

She lives with her husband (who talks less than she does) and her three cats, who always talk back.

Stay in Touch

ALSO BY BONNIE ELIZABETH

THE FROST WITCH SAGA

October Snow

November Frost

December Storm

APPALACHIAN SOULS

Souls Lost

Souls Broken

THE ASH JERICHO SERIES

An Inheritance to Die For

A Discovery to Die For

A Distraction to Die For

THE WHISPER NOVELS

Whisper Bound

Taken by the Sound

An Air of Suspicion

Little Dog Lost

Death Interrupted

Down in Whisper

A Haunting Whisper

A Haunting Attraction

Secrets Not Whispers

Only Human

OTHER NOVELS

One Bad Wish

Sun Spot Magic

Ghosts from the Past

Unnatural Secrets

Shadows of Solstice

Find them all at your favorite bookseller or check us out at
MyBigFatOrangeCat.com